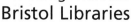
Paul Stewart was born in London. Before becoming a full-time writer, Paul taught English as a foreign language in Germany and Sri Lanka, and travelled extensively throughout Europe and Asia, Kenya, New England and Australia. Paul is also a graduate of the renowned creative writing course at the University of East Anglia, studying with Malcolm Bradbury and Angela Carter. Paul is probably best known as the co-author, with artist Chris Riddell, of the hugely popular _Edge Chronicles_. His work has been published in over twenty languages and his novel _The Wakening_ was selected as a Pick of the Year by the Federation of Children's Book Groups. His recent books, _The Blobheads_, have been made into a TV series for Nickelodeon.

Paul works every single day of the year, apart from Christmas day, from his home in Brighton.

USBORNE THRILLERS

Terry Deary
The Boy Who Haunted Himself

Ann Evans
The Beast

Sandra Glover
Demon's Rock

Malcolm Rose
The Tortured Wood

The Curse of Magoria

PAUL STEWART

USBORNE

For Anna

———————————————

First published in 2004 by Usborne Publishing Ltd., Usborne House,
83-85 Saffron Hill, London EC1N 8RT, England. www.usborne.com

A CIP catalogue record for this book is available from the British Library.

JFMAMJJASON /10 00571/1   ISBN 9780746062326
Printed in Chippenham, Eastbourne, UK.

Chapter One

Greetings

Ryan Schilling stepped down onto the deserted platform of Steinfeld Station. It was bitterly cold after the warmth of the compartment. When he breathed in, the freezing air hurt his nose and lungs. When he breathed out, thick coils of mist wrapped themselves around his head. There wasn't a soul in sight.

His Uncle Karl had said he'd be there to meet him at the station. So where was he?

Ryan picked up his backpack and headed for the empty ticket barrier, hoping to find someone outside. He hadn't gone more than half a dozen steps when a huge dog skidded into view. It looked up, sniffed the air and, barking furiously, came hurtling across the platform at him.

Ryan froze. He wasn't a fan of dogs at the best of times, and this one was a *monster*. It was big and obviously strong, with a thick white coat and cold black eyes. As it got closer it opened its slobbering jaws. Ryan found himself staring at two rows of glistening, razor-sharp teeth.

He groaned. Not two minutes off the train and already he'd come face to face with the hound from hell.

Ryan backed away, his heart racing. The dog launched itself into the air, its outstretched claws lunging up at him. He raised his backpack protectively and rammed it between the creature's gaping jaws.

As its teeth sank into the bag, the dog's paws thumped against Ryan's chest and sent him flying through the air. He landed with a heavy bump – at the very edge of the platform.

He looked up at the dog standing over him. Now that it had caught him, it seemed in no particular hurry to finish Ryan off.

"Gooood doggy!" Ryan cooed, optimistically.

He saw the dog's ears prick up, and it turned and looked round. Then Ryan heard it too – the sound of footsteps echoing from the ticket hall, followed by a man's voice.

"Max!" it roared. "Heel, boy!"

The owner, thought Ryan. At last. But, ignoring the man's yells, the dog lowered its head. The vicious jaws parted. Ryan closed his eyes.

He felt warm breath on his face and with it the stench of rotten meat.

"MAX!" the man bellowed, and Ryan heard him hurrying across the platform.

Ryan flinched as the dog's wet, warm, and very rough tongue lapped at his chin, and up over his nose. He was being *tasted*.

The next instant, there was an abrupt jolt, and the weight on his chest disappeared.

"Ryan?" he heard. "It is you, isn't it?"

Ryan looked up. Standing there was a tall man with straw-like hair and bright blue eyes. Ryan recognized him from numerous snapshots. It was Uncle Karl – but, unlike his smiling pictures, this real Uncle Karl had a concerned look on his face.

"I'm so sorry," he said, helping Ryan to his feet. "Max doesn't usually behave like that. He must have been very excited about meeting you."

Ryan looked at the dog. With its wagging tail and lolling tongue, it – *he* – looked friendly now. All the same, Ryan was glad that his uncle had a firm hold on his collar.

*

Three days earlier it had been Ryan's birthday. Months before that, his parents had promised him an extra special birthday present. He was to stay with his Uncle Karl and Aunt Ingrid.

Ryan had been looking forward to the trip for ages. Most importantly, he would be visiting the country where his dad had grown up, and meeting his dad's brother face to face for the first time. It would also give him a chance to use his German, and maybe even learn to ski.

The journey had been an exciting one; all the more so for going by himself. The plane flight, the train trip, everything had gone without a hitch. And now here he was, only a car ride from Oberdorf where Uncle Karl and Aunt Ingrid lived, in the house where his dad had been born.

"I apologize for not being here on time," said his uncle. "The weather's suddenly turned. It's snowing heavily up in the mountains and the drive down here took longer than I expected."

"That's okay," said Ryan. He looked up at the sky. It was a curdled yellow-grey.

"It's strange," said Uncle Karl, picking up Ryan's backpack. "There was no mention of bad weather on the TV this morning, and our weather forecasts are usually pretty accurate. The snow clouds just seemed to come from nowhere...probably about the time you crossed the border."

They began walking to the station exit, with Max straining at the leash.

"We'd better get a move on," said his uncle as they crossed the car park together. "It'll be snowing down here soon, and it's going to get a lot worse higher up the mountain."

"The way Dad talks, it never stops snowing in Oberdorf," said Ryan.

His uncle smiled. "Your dad always did like to exaggerate. There's always *some* snow in the mountains in the winter, but that doesn't mean it snows *all* the time...and we usually get some warning." They reached a large four-wheel drive vehicle. It was the only car in the car park.

Uncle Karl clapped his hand on his nephew's shoulder. "It's good to meet you at last, Ryan," he said. "It's such a shame your father's job seems to take him everywhere in the world – except here! Your Aunt Ingrid is very excited about your visit too," he added. "Let's get home."

They pulled out of the car park just as the first snow began to fall on the town of Steinfeld.

Chapter Two

Storm Brewing

By the time they'd reached the outskirts of town, it was impossible to see where the edge of the road was. Despite the snowchains Uncle Karl had put on the wheels, the going was tough – even for a four-wheel drive. Ryan peered up out of the passenger window and watched the grey and yellow clouds swirling dizzily across the sky.

"I can't understand it," Uncle Karl commented. "Nothing like this showed up on the satellite pictures." They set off once more.

"Is this a *real* blizzard?" asked Ryan.

His uncle didn't answer immediately. His eyes were fixed on the road ahead. "It could be. We do get them," he said, at last. "But some are worse than others. When I was your age, Oberdorf was cut off by snow for almost two weeks and, eighty years ago or so, eighteen people died when—"

"But that couldn't happen now, could it?" said Ryan. "Not with helicopters and computers and things?"

Uncle Karl shook his head thoughtfully. "I certainly hope not," he said. "But nature can still catch us off guard."

He turned the car onto the road to Oberdorf. The wipers had to struggle hard against the snow driving straight at the windscreen. It was getting thicker and thicker by the minute.

Ryan stared out of the side window. "I never realized snow could be so dangerous," he said.

"Five people died up on the glacier last year," said Uncle Karl. "They were skiing off-piste on a clear day when they were suddenly hit by an avalanche. But there won't be any skiing in this weather. The lifts won't be running..." He paused. "I've never seen the snow so thick on this stretch of road before."

Slowly, blindly, they made their way along the narrow road which snaked its way through the trees, hairpin bend after hairpin bend, up the mountainside. Ryan found himself gripping the seat. He peered out of the passenger window, through the swirling mass of snow. Beyond the white edges of the road was a sheer drop that fell away to nothing. Ryan could feel his heart beating rapidly. Behind him, at the back of the car, Max whimpered unhappily.

Ryan glanced at his uncle who was hunched over the wheel, a frown of concentration on his face. "How far is Oberdorf now?" he asked nervously.

"It should only take ten minutes from here," said Uncle Karl. "Though heaven knows how long we'll be in this."

Ryan looked through the side window again. Black tree trunks, white snow; the whole landscape had turned to monochrome. As they rounded one particularly sharp bend they saw a van parked up ahead. A man was on all fours struggling with snowchains on the wheels. Uncle Karl had to steer his way carefully around the van, taking the car perilously near the edge.

Suddenly, Ryan felt the car lose control. His stomach lurched and he could imagine all four wheels spinning powerlessly. He closed his eyes. They were sliding sideways – closer and closer to the sheer drop over the edge of the road.

Uncle Karl said nothing. The next instant, Ryan heard a reassuring crunch as the chains on the wheels gripped the surface. When he opened his eyes again, they had left the van well behind them.

They drove on in silence. The road curved and twisted its way up and up to the little mountain village of Oberdorf. The only sound was the rhythmic thud of the snowchains biting into the drifting snow.

It was darker now and Uncle Karl switched the headlights to full beam. Ryan stared ahead, mesmerized by the glittering snow, which danced in the broad wedges of light. It looked like a vast swarm of white bees.

The road began to flatten out and Ryan was glad to see trees on both sides of the road. In the distance, he could just make out the shapes of rooftops and chimneys and a glimmer of light. Without warning, Uncle Karl turned left up a steep narrow track through the trees – a track that Ryan hadn't even noticed was there.

The car crept on at a snail's pace until they reached a clearing where the track ended. Through the snow, Ryan saw a wooden house with a steep, tiled roof. He recognized it at once. This was the house his dad had told him so much about – the house on the edge of a tall, dark forest. Right now it was impossible to make out the trees of the forest, or anything else for that matter. The snow was deep all round and in places it had drifted almost up to the windows.

"Here at last," said Uncle Karl with a sigh of relief. "And I'm not going out again tonight...not for anything!"

Ryan stepped out of the car, into thick, deep snow that came up to his knees. The cold hit him with a blast as a sudden gust of wind caught the car door and seized it from his grasp. The snowflakes seemed to whip themselves into a frenzied flurry, lashing at his body and stinging his face.

The windows of the house gave off a warm glow. Ryan noticed that someone had cleared the drifting snow from the front door, but it was already starting to build up again.

The door opened and a woman stood framed in light. Ryan didn't recognize her at first. In real life Aunt Ingrid looked softer and plumper than she did in photographs. And right now she was also looking worried. Ryan waded through the snow towards her.

"Come in! Come in!" Aunt Ingrid called out in slightly accented English. "What weather we are having to greet you, Ryan."

Max jumped down from the car into a heap of snow. He shook himself, and sniffed the air. He seemed wary, and was whimpering again. "What's wrong, boy?" asked Uncle Karl, obviously surprised by the dog's antics. In the distance, a clock chimed. For a brief moment, despite the comforting smell of wood smoke and cooking coming through the open door, Ryan shivered with unease.

He watched as Max's fur bristled and his ears went flat. The dog raised his head and howled. The desperate cry seemed to hang in the air and was followed by an eerie, distant echo before it was swallowed up by the snow.

Chapter Three

Cut off

It was liver dumplings for supper. Ryan's dad was always going on about liver dumplings and how much he'd liked them as a boy. Now, for the first time, Ryan could taste them for himself. He'd always thought that liver was bad enough – but with dumplings... *yuck*, disgusting.

They turned out to be delicious. As he finished his third bowlful, Ryan's eyelids began to grow heavy. The warmth of the large kitchen was almost enough to block out all thought of the terrible weather outside. He yawned. It had been a long and exciting day.

"Why don't you go up to bed, if you're tired?"

suggested his aunt. "We've put you in the little room right at the top of the house. It was your father's. In fact, I think it's the same bed, though it must have had a new mattress since then!"

"Great," said Ryan.

Ryan's dad, Peter Schilling, was born in Oberdorf and had lived there until he went abroad to work. It was then that he'd met Ryan's mother. That was twenty years ago. They married and, later, Ryan was born. Peter hadn't been back to Oberdorf in all that time.

Aunt Ingrid looked at Ryan. "You would like to phone your parents before going to bed, Ryan?" she asked, bustling him into the hall. "To let them know you've arrived safely."

Ryan picked up the phone. It was dead.

"What's the matter?" asked Aunt Ingrid, taking the receiver from him. She tutted irritably. "Karl," she called out. "The phone's not working."

"It's the weather," said Uncle Karl, appearing from the kitchen. Ryan was suddenly aware of the wind rattling at the shutters and buffeting the doors. "The lines must have come down. They'll fix them when it stops snowing."

"You can try the mobile," said Ryan's aunt. She left the room and returned with a mobile phone, which she handed to Ryan.

That didn't work either.

"That's odd," said Uncle Karl. "I just charged the battery. Maybe it's the weather interfering with the signal. Still, it can't be helped. You'll just have to try again in the morning."

Ryan smiled. "Okay," he said. "Goodnight."

"Goodnight, Ryan," said his uncle and aunt. "Pleasant dreams!"

Ryan turned and looked back. "Thanks," he said, but – for a fleeting moment and for no obvious reason – the strange feeling of unease he'd felt outside returned. But everything was so *nice* here; so cosy. I'm just tired, he thought.

The bedroom was just as his father had described it. There was a low, sloping ceiling and, instead of curtains, closed shutters beyond the windows kept out the light. On the wall, a cuckoo clock ticked softly. Ryan undressed quickly, switched off the lamp and slid under a billowing white cotton quilt.

The wind continued to whistle and whine outside. Downstairs, Max howled again and again. It was only when he was finally silenced by one last, furious *"Quiet, Max!"* from Uncle Karl, that Ryan heard the other desperate cries. It was as if every dog in Oberdorf had been upset by something.

Was it the weather? Or was there something else?

Ryan pulled the quilt around his ears to shut out the noise. He thought of his dad as a child, tucked up warm and snug in the same soft, downy bed. His eyes closed and he drifted off, almost at once, into a deep, dark sleep. "Pleasant dreams", they'd said, and a pleasant dream he had...to begin with.

As the night went on, however, the sound of the snowstorm filtered into Ryan's thoughts. Little by little, the dream turned into a nightmare.

Chapter Four

The Nightmare

Ryan sat in an empty compartment of a train. He was on his way to Steinfeld, on his way to Uncle Karl, on his way to the place where his father was born. He had to get off soon. Station after station went past, but the train didn't stop. The train couldn't stop.

On and on it went, plunging ever deeper into a dense forest. Ryan looked out through a giddy swirl of snow, down at the sheer drop that fell away to nothing at the side of the track.

A moment later, he found himself in the corridor, lurching and bumping past endless empty compartments. Suddenly, a locked door loomed up in *front of him. The front of the train. Red letters on a huge sign flashed on and off, pulsing out a message:*

Ryan's head was filled with the sound of a rhythmic thump that seemed to grow faster and faster...a shrill squeal of metal as the wheels sped on. He stumbled. Arms flailing, he hurtled towards the door...and simply passed right through it into the driver's cab. It was empty. Huge letters flashed before his eyes:

Ryan looked for the brake but saw buttons instead. Red buttons, blue buttons, green buttons...but which button would stop the train?

The forest rushed past the window in a dark blur, stirred up with a frenzy of snow. He was hurtling down a never-ending tunnel. And all the while, the pine needles scratched and scraped at the window, and the cold snow stung his face.

"This is only a dream," Ryan told himself. But he couldn't wake up.

The train was gone. Ryan was in the forest. Afraid and alone. "This is only a dream. I must wake up. This is only a dream..." But he could feel the cold. He could hear the snow crunching beneath his feet. He could see his misty breath coiling in the shadowy moonlight...and he somehow knew that he was being hunted. All that mattered was escape.

Ryan stumbled blindly through the thick undergrowth. Pine needles slashed at his face, barbed thorns snagged his clothes and gnarled roots tripped him...but on he went. Then he heard the mournful sound of a howling wolf; of a hundred howling wolves... No escape.

The forest grew thicker, as thick as a hedge. Down he went on hands and knees, crawling along. "Escape, you must escape. This is only a dream..."

All of a sudden he was in a clearing, thick with snow, on the edge of a tall, dark forest. And straight ahead was a row of burning, yellow eyes.

He opened his mouth to scream, but no sound would come. He turned to run, but his legs were stuck. The yellow eyes stared out of the darkness and grew before his eyes.

Suddenly, he was face to face with a monstrous

beast with a thick white coat and cold yellow eyes. Ryan backed away. The wolf launched itself into the air, its yellow fangs bared...

Ryan raised his arms as the hot, rotten breath hit him in the face and he fell back, flying through the air over a white pile of snow, back over the edge and down a sheer drop...

He landed on something cold and smooth and hard. He turned his head and looked up. He was sitting at the foot of a marble staircase that led all the way up the outside of a tall tower...a tower which pointed to the sky like a black marble finger. A bell tolled far above him.

It was a clock tower.

Then Ryan was halfway up a flight of spiral stairs, winding around the outside of the tower like a helter skelter... No escape.

Up and up he climbed without the slightest effort. The walls, as smooth as glass, reflected a second Ryan climbing up beside him. Up and up and up... Suddenly, the stairs came to a halt. He was facing a blank wall of marble. The wolves howled far below. No door. No escape. Above him, the top of the clock tower disappeared into the clouds.

"And no way to get up there," he found himself saying.

"Oh, yes there is," came a voice. It was his reflection; it was talking to him!

"I'm dreaming," said Ryan. "This is a dream."

"Then wake up," the reflection told him. "Are you coming in or not?" it demanded. It reached out with its hand.

Ryan stretched out his own hand...and was yanked abruptly through the solid marble wall and into the tower, where the staircase continued into the gloom.

Up he went, step after marble step. A pale, gloomy glow was coming in through narrow slits in the walls. "No escape," he panted. "No escape."

Now Ryan was in a dark passageway, so low and narrow he had to continue on his knees. It was dark. He couldn't see a thing.

And the air...

There was no air.

It was getting harder and harder...to...breathe...

Growing desperate, he felt his way around the smooth walls, hoping to find some kind of concealed doorway. But there was none. The cold, hard slabs all refused to budge.

No escape.

I'll have to go back. I must go back.

But he couldn't go back. There was no room to turn and, no matter where Ryan stretched his arms and legs, he struck the wall. It was a trap. It had been a trap all along... He was stuck inside a black marble coffin.

"Help," he cried out.

"HELP?" boomed a disembodied voice. "YOU COME INSIDE THE TOWER WITHOUT PERMISSION," it cried. "AND NOW YOU ASK FOR HELP?"

"But I didn't know..."

"YOUR IGNORANCE IS OF NO CONCERN TO ME," the voice retorted. "YOU ARE HERE AND HERE YOU SHALL REMAIN."

Ryan clawed frantically at the walls. He must escape. He must...

He must...

The voice was speaking again, so loudly that the black marble itself vibrated.

"THERE'S NO ESCAPE...NO ESCAPE..NO ESCAPE," it bellowed, the words echoing away to nothing.

No escape.

"This is only a dream," Ryan kept on telling himself. "Only a dream."

Chapter Five

Emergency!

Ryan woke with a start. He opened his eyes and stifled a scream. He couldn't see, he couldn't move – he could scarcely even breathe. He was still trapped inside the black marble coffin...

Then he realized that the "ceiling" just above him was soft and warm. It was only the quilt! He kicked it off.

His body wet with sweat, he lay still for a moment, his breathing fast and shallow as relief flooded through him.

He sat up in bed. He'd had nightmares before, but this was different. The events were still clear in his mind; every move, every sound – the train, the wolf, the tolling bell, the clock tower pointing to the sky like a black marble finger, and the disembodied voice.

And although he was awake now, and surrounded by the comforting presence of his father's old room, the fear he'd felt was still with him, lurking somewhere just below the surface. Ryan shivered. The memory of being walled up inside the clock tower was terrifyingly real.

He climbed out of bed, pulled on his clothes and padded across the room. He fumbled with the latch and pulled open the window. He tried to open the shutters. At first, they wouldn't budge. Then, with a swoosh-*flupp* the snow on the window ledge slipped down into the drift below, the shutters flew back, and the room was filled with dazzling sunshine.

Ryan looked around. Everything was white, softly rounded, and twinkling in the bright sunlight. It was like looking down on clouds from an aircraft, though without the drone of its engine. All was silent. The wind was still, the dogs were quiet and not a single bird sang.

It was bitterly cold and Ryan reached to shut the windows again. The sound of bells shattering the silence froze his movements. They were like the bells he'd heard in his dream. One, two, three, four...

For a split second, the sky seemed to tear apart – ripping in two like blue canvas being slashed with a knife.

Ryan found himself staring, mesmerized, at the rip, then *through* it into the yawning blackness beyond. The next moment – as abruptly as it had opened – the sky closed up again, like an instantly healed wound. In the distance, the bells continued to chime. Six, seven...

Ryan went hurtling down the stairs and collided with his uncle at the bottom. "Uncle Karl—" he blurted.

"In a minute, Ryan," said his uncle. "Things are worse than I thought."

"But the sky!" Ryan panted.

"I know, it's clear again," said Uncle Karl, "but the snow's a nightmare. It's drifted up to the rooftops in some places and not even the snow-clearing equipment can get through."

"But—"

"The telephone lines are down, the mobile's still not working, and even the computer's on the blink," his uncle went on, steering Ryan into the kitchen. "We're cut off. The whole of Oberdorf is cut off."

Aunt Ingrid looked up from the table as they entered the room. "Good morning, Ryan," she said with a tired smile. "Did you sleep well? Sit down. Sit down."

Laid out on the table in front of him was salami, ham, cheese, bread rolls, coffee and orange juice. Despite the fire, he felt cold and shivery.

Ryan was beginning to wonder whether he'd imagined what he'd just seen in the sky; whether his mind had been playing tricks after his nightmare – or perhaps it had something to do with this crazy weather. He felt calmer sitting with his aunt and uncle, not that what they were discussing was good news.

"I wonder how the people farther up the mountain are coping, Karl," said Aunt Ingrid. "If the snow's this deep down here, I dread to think what it must be like for them."

"We'll have to find out," said Uncle Karl grimly.

"Isn't there anything about it on the radio or television?" asked Ryan.

"Who knows?" said his uncle. "They're as dead as everything else. I guess it's some kind of climatic interference." He shook his head. "I've never known anything this bad."

"I don't like it, Karl," said Aunt Ingrid.

Uncle Karl saw the worried look on Ryan's face and gave a broad grin. "Well, we'll just have to do the best we can, because there's no escape for the time being!" he said, giving Ryan a friendly squeeze of the shoulders. "Now eat up. If you're anything like your dad was at your age, you'll polish this off in no time."

But Ryan's mind wasn't on breakfast. No escape, his uncle had said. His whole nightmare had been about trying to escape...and failing, time after time.

No escape. Those were the very words spoken by that strange voice with the power to vibrate the black marble walls that entombed him. *No escape*. The words that had haunted his sleep.

Pull yourself together, thought Ryan, taking a swig of orange juice. It was only a stupid dream. There were some far more important things to be thinking about.

"We need a plan of action," his uncle was saying. "For a start, there's that package for Marta." He nodded over to a brown paper parcel lying in the corner of the room. "It's marked *urgent*," he explained. "Anyway, we ought to make sure that she's okay. If you could deliver it, Ingrid, I'll go and make sure that old Geisselhardt and his wife are all right. Take Max with you."

Aunt Ingrid nodded. "I'll heat up some soup," she said. "You know how much she loves my—"

At that moment, there was a loud knock at the

front door. Uncle Karl went to answer it.

"Daniel!" he said to a small man muffled up in an old coat and a huge hat with ear flaps. The coat was buttoned up to the neck and appeared to be straining at every seam from the number of sweaters underneath. "What's the latest?"

"Bad news, I'm afraid," said the man. "It's the Stock family. Hans is away on business, Eva's about to have her baby and there's no way of bringing her down to the hospital in Steinfeld or of getting the doctor to her."

"We'll have to get over to her at once," said Aunt Ingrid.

Uncle Karl agreed. "Tell them we're on our way, Daniel," he said. The man nodded and left.

In the flurry of activity that followed, Ryan was all but forgotten. It was only when the time came for them to leave that Uncle Karl turned to him.

"I'm sorry, Ryan. Your aunt and I think you'd better stay here," he said. "The conditions out there are treacherous. Your parents wouldn't thank us if we sent you home with frostbite."

"I understand," sighed Ryan, trying not to look too disappointed. He'd have liked to be a part of the action. And what on earth would he do all by himself in the house?

"We'll leave you Max for company," his uncle added. Ryan wasn't sure that was such a good idea, but he didn't feel he could say so. He just hoped the dog would behave without his master and mistress around.

Even though it still wasn't working, Uncle Karl decided to take his mobile with him. "Might get a signal higher up," he said, as he pushed it into his pocket and opened the front door. Aunt Ingrid followed him out.

"Good luck," said Ryan brightly. Yet, as he watched them setting off across the featureless white landscape in their bright red padded jackets, he felt a tight knot in the pit of his stomach. He hoped they'd be okay.

With nowhere to go, Ryan took the opportunity to explore the house. It didn't take long. Although there were lots of rooms, several were empty.

The room next to his attic bedroom contained a computer. Ryan looked at it and whistled. It was fantastic: huge screen, scanner, laser printer, CD-ROM, modem... It looked as though it should be able to do anything. He sat down at the desk and switched it on.

The computer coughed and whirred, and a blizzard of snowy interference filled the screen. Uncle

Karl was right. It did seem to be on the blink. Ryan turned it off again, but the screen stayed on...and the snowy interference began to form shapes. Ryan watched with fascination.

First a semicircle appeared, then a circle – and another circle. Finally, a jagged line zigzagged its way across the screen. Ryan gasped. It was forming letters. They were crude, but there was no doubt what they were spelling out:

DOOM

Ryan felt very uneasy. Even his uncle wouldn't be able to blame *this* on the weather. Could there be more unusual things happening in Oberdorf than just a freak blizzard?

Back downstairs, the brown paper package in the corner of the kitchen caught his eye. *Urgent* his uncle had said. He went across and took a closer look. The parcel was tied up with string and addressed to:

FRÄULEIN M. MARTINE,
DAS BLOCKHAUS,
DUNKELWALD,
OBERDORF.

"Miss M. Martine, The Log Cabin, Dark Wood," Ryan translated.

When news of the Stock family had arrived, poor old Marta Martine had been forgotten. And, in Ryan's book, urgent meant urgent. It occurred to him that *he* could deliver the package.

Of course, he knew that his aunt and uncle had expressly advised him not to leave the house. The conditions outside were treacherous. But surely, if he could lay his hands on a map, he should be able to find the address easily enough. Besides, it had sounded as though the pair of them would be gone for ages. If he set off soon, he could be there and back before they returned.

After some searching, he found a map in a kitchen drawer, together with a compass, a flashlight and a Swiss Army knife.

He laid the map out on the kitchen table, and saw that the *Blockhaus* had been marked in pen. It was in the forest just north of the village and – assuming the map was right – there was a track just behind the house which would lead him directly to it.

Perfect, Ryan thought. It was on a path, so he shouldn't get lost and, with any luck, the snow wouldn't be so thick in the forest, under the cover of the pine trees.

"Anyway," he said to himself, trying hard to ignore the shivers of unease which tingled up and down his spine, "I'll have Max with me. Everything will be fine."

Chapter Six

Into the Forest

Ten minutes later Ryan was ready to go. He left a scribbled note on the table to say where he had gone, just in case, and stuffed the parcel into his slightly chewed backpack. With fumbling fingers, he clipped the leash on Max's collar. Then, taking a last gulp of warm air, he opened the back door.

Outside, the snow had drifted into huge piles beside the house. He could see tracks, probably made by his aunt or uncle...deep holes in the thick, white snow. It was numbingly cold.

"We're going to Marta Martine's house," he said to the dog. "It could be a matter of life and dea—"

The moment Max heard the woman's name, he pulled the leash from Ryan's hand, jumped into the snow and disappeared up to his neck. Ryan smiled and gingerly stepped out after him. The snow went up to his thighs. It was slow work covering the short distance to the forest edge.

Just as he'd hoped, the snow wasn't nearly as deep in the forest – only up to his ankles and fairly easy to walk through. What he hadn't counted on was how steep the track would be. With Max bounding along in front of him, he was soon short of breath.

"Heel, boy," he shouted hopefully, remembering how disobedient the dog had been at the station. This time, though, Max did as he was told. Ryan grabbed the leash and Max trotted along at his side.

"Good dog," he said, and cautiously stroked his head and neck. Max looked around and licked Ryan's glove.

As the pair of them went deeper into the silent forest, Ryan shuddered. The snow-covered branches of the pine trees high above his head cut out the light and cast dark shadows across the forest floor. The deeper they went, the thicker the trees grew.

Barbed thorns. Knotted roots. Everything seemed ominously familiar. The rocks, the branches, even the track itself. It was as if he'd been here before...

Telling himself he was being silly, Ryan nevertheless scanned the shadows for any telltale glints of yellow eyes. Of course there weren't any wolves, not in this forest. Max was wagging his tail happily enough, so there couldn't possibly be any, but...but...

Ryan quickened his pace. As they trotted through the trees, sometimes Ryan led the way, sometimes Max overtook him. On and on they went, hurrying up the mountainside until finally – gasping for breath and exhausted – the pair of them emerged in a clearing.

Ryan looked up. Ahead of him, a little log cabin nestled in the thick snow. It was like something out of a fairytale – inviting, almost beautiful, yet, for some strange reason, oddly sinister.

"Come on, boy," said Ryan, uneasily. "Let's deliver this package and get back home again."

He removed the parcel from his backpack, and knocked lightly on the dark wooden door. It flew open almost at once and Ryan found himself face to face with an old woman, no taller than himself.

"Was willst du?" she snapped. Her voice was harsh and rasping.

Ryan tried not to stare, but it was hard not to. The woman's hair was a mass of dyed golden curls;

her face so heavily made up that it was like looking at a mask. A very angry mask. Ryan held out the package. "This is for you," he said nervously.

The woman seized the parcel with gnarled fingers and tore at the paper. Inside was a green tin. "Excellent!" she said, a broad smile spreading across her bright red lips. She spoke English with such a heavy accent that Ryan could barely understand her. "Come in. Come in." She stepped aside to let him enter.

Ryan hung back, reluctant to step inside. "Actually, I should be getting back," he said.

"Nonsense. Come in," said the old woman, extending a bony hand and placing it on his arm. "You're not from around here," she said, making it sound like an accusation.

"No," he said. "I'm Ryan Schilling. I'm staying with my aunt and uncle –"

"Of course," said the woman, looking down at Max who was strangely silent at Ryan's side. "Dear Ingrid and Karl. I thought I recognized Max. You will stay, won't you?"

The words were friendly enough, but the way she said them was so creepy. Or perhaps it's just the way she looks, thought Ryan. Her dark red lips and golden hair made him think of a plastic doll's head stuck onto an old crone's body.

There was something not right here. But despite Ryan's misgivings, Max clearly felt at home. He trotted through the door and settled down in the outer lobby.

He's obviously been here before and lived to tell the tale, thought Ryan. I'm just being stupid. He followed reluctantly and Miss Martine closed the door behind them and bolted it.

"To stop it rattling in the wind," she explained. "Now, come and warm yourself by the fire. I'll put some water on to boil."

The little wooden house was hot and airless, and smelled of stale perfume and stewed tea. It was also so jam-packed full of furniture, objects and ornaments that there was barely room to turn around.

The walls of the hallway were lined with framed black and white photographs; stills of characters from old movies.

As he looked more closely, Ryan realized that the beautiful woman in every photo was the same person. It was only the make-up and costumes that were different. Then he recognized the steely glint in her eyes. The pictures were all of Miss Martine herself – as she had been a long time ago. A very long time ago.

"Yes," came her voice from behind him. Ryan

nearly jumped out of his skin. "I was once a movie star. These are some of my greatest roles." She grabbed Ryan's arm and pulled him across to a framed newspaper clipping.

"MARTA MARTINE: 'QUEEN OF THE SCREEN' RETIRES"

the headlines announced. It was dated 17th November, 1967.

"That was me," she said with pride. "I may have kept my screen name, but my destiny lies here in the heart of the forest. All that fame and fortune is behind me now."

Ryan's eyes flitted past the newspaper clipping. Suddenly, he froze.

There was one picture that was very different from all the rest. It was an old-fashioned black and white print. A woodcut...a woodcut of a building that Ryan recognized at once. The square tower, the spiral staircase, the ornate carvings – pointing to the sky, like a black marble finger. It was the clock tower from his nightmare.

Chapter Seven
The Voice

"That picture," gasped Ryan, pointing at it with a slightly unsteady finger. "Is that from one of your films?"

Marta Martine glared at him. "No," she said. "Why do you ask?"

"I don't know..." Ryan hesitated.

"Yes you do. Tell me," continued the old woman. "You recognize it, don't you?"

"No," Ryan protested. "Not really. I mean, I dreamed about it. That's all."

"You dreamed of the Clock of Doom?" she asked in a curious voice.

The Clock of *Doom*? The words hit him like a brick.

Ryan stared at the ancient picture of the clock tower, remembering the touch of the cool, smooth marble, recalling the steps he'd climbed...the dark passageway...the walls closing in around him...

This was stupid. It was only a dream. "Why is it called the Clock of Doom?" he asked.

"Because that's what it is," said Marta Martine. "It might look like an ordinary clock tower on the outside, but it's what's on the inside that makes it so...so *special*."

"You've been inside it?" asked Ryan. He pictured the nightmare image of the cold, hard slabs all around him. No way forward. No way back. *No escape.*

"Oh no," laughed the old woman, harshly. "No one has seen the Clock of Doom, not for centuries... Except, it seems, for you."

"I told you, it was just a dream," Ryan said. It was getting stuffier in the strange-smelling hallway.

"Just a dream?" Miss Martine repeated. She fixed him with her steely blue eyes. "Sometimes dreams hold more truth than you realize." She gripped his arm once more. "Come with me. You must tell me everything."

Ryan shook his head warily. "I really ought to be

getting back," he said. "Aunt Ingrid will be—"

"Come!" she repeated.

Suddenly, Ryan's head began to fill with the sound of distant ticking. Soft at first, it grew louder and louder – until it was hammering deafeningly inside his head. Ryan clamped his hands to his ears.

The old woman stood back. Max whimpered.

Out of the throbbing din inside his head came a voice. *"Help me,"* it said. *"You must help me."*

The voice – an old man's voice – was weak and faltering and it was speaking *inside Ryan's mind*.

And then it was gone.

"What is it, Ryan?" demanded another voice. "What is it? Are you all right?" Miss Martine was shaking him.

"Y-Yes. I'm all right, thank you."

Miss Martine steered him into a cluttered sitting room and sat him down in a red velvet armchair. She sat opposite him, crossing her legs and clasping her leathery hands together around one knee.

"What happened just then?" she demanded.

"Nothing... I mean, I'm not sure..."

"Tell me," said Miss Martine through narrowed lips.

"I know this sounds crazy," said Ryan. "But I thought I heard a voice inside my head."

His extraordinary hostess fixed his gaze with hers. "Ryan Schilling," she said, sternly. "You haven't come here to play tricks on an old lady, have you?"

"No," Ryan protested.

"I suppose you're going to tell me next that you've never heard the legend?" she said. "Are you trying to make a fool of me? First you claim to have dreamed of the Clock of Doom and now you talk of hearing strange voices."

"I promise you," said Ryan, "I'd never heard of the Clock of Doom until now." He didn't like the steely tone that had crept into Miss Martine's voice, or the slightly crazed look in her eyes. He was wondering how he could collect Max and get out through the front door without seeming *too* rude. "I never knew it existed until I saw your picture – and *you* told me its name."

Marta Martine put her face right up to his. He could smell a mixture of perfume and the make-up caked to her leathery skin. She stared into his eyes. "I believe you," she said at last. "I knew this day would come. The day when the Clock decided to take its revenge."

Ryan looked down at his feet, embarrassed by the old woman's talk. What was she ranting about now? She's nuts, he thought. Bonkers.

"As I said, the Clock of Doom is no ordinary clock," she told him. "Ordinary clocks measure and record the passing of time. The Clock of Doom, on the other hand, was built for quite a different purpose." She looked away.

"Really?" said Ryan. She was beginning to sound how Ryan imagined a character in one of her old films might have spoken; theatrical, overdramatic.

Marta looked up. "The Clock was designed to *control* time."

Max whimpered in the outer lobby, and a plaintive wail reached Ryan's ears. It grew louder and louder and became a high-pitched whistle. Ryan's skin prickled.

"That'll be the kettle," said his hostess, getting to her feet. "I'll be back in a moment."

Of course, it was only a whistling kettle. What else could it have been? Ryan watched Miss Martine leave the room.

He moved closer to the fire, and looked up at a row of shelves crammed full of books of myths, fairytales and legends.

The old woman returned with a steaming mug in each hand.

"The coffee you brought me," she explained, putting one of the mugs on the arm of his chair.

"Coffee? What coffee?" asked Ryan.

"The coffee in the package," she said.

"You mean that's all it was? I thought it was urgent –"

"You should see me without my coffee," she chuckled. She sat back down and sipped the steaming brew. "Heaven," she purred.

Ryan laughed. The spell was broken. This was no witch in the woods. This was an elderly woman who'd once been a movie star, but had lost her looks and wore too much make-up. Sure, she had a strange way of talking, but she was just a little batty; that was all.

"Please tell me more about the Clock of Doom," he said.

"I'll do better than that," she said. "You can read about it yourself. I always knew that it was more than a legend." She headed for one of the bookshelves. "It's in a book with a red cover... Aah, here we are."

Marta Martine took down an old, worn leather-bound book and flipped through the pages.

"Here we are," she said at last.

Ryan took the heavy volume carefully.

The page was open at an illustration that Ryan immediately recognized. It was the tower from his nightmare. Ryan shuddered. He turned the page and began to read: "The Legend of the Clock of Doom..."

Chapter Eight

The Legend of the Clock of Doom

Once upon a time, long, long ago, in the Kingdom of Alpenpfalz, there lived a sorcerer by the name of Magoria the Mathemagician. He was a great wizard with vast knowledge and mighty powers. He knew the secret of numbers, and the hidden powers of earth, air, fire and water. Heavy magic hung around him like a fog.

Like all sorcerers, Magoria had an apprentice to help him with his work. This man, named Wytchwood, came from a distant land and, though he lacked Magoria's magical powers, he had far greater wisdom than his master.

Alpenpfalz, a small but wealthy kingdom in the mountains, was ruled by a prince who built a splendid palace at Oberdorf. His desire was to fill this royal home with strange wonders that would be the envy of other kingdoms.

It was to Magoria the Mathemagician that the prince turned for help. In return, the grateful prince invited the sorcerer to help him rule his kingdom. Magoria jumped at the opportunity, and soon the air around the palace was thick with magic.

People would come from far and wide to see the latest wonders that the prince had on show: a flying machine, a floating garden, fiery balls that illuminated every room, and fountains that never stopped and never froze.

To the prince, these were simply wonders to behold. To Magoria, however, they represented the height of his magical powers and his mastery over the elements.

Then, one day, a peasant farmer brought Magoria an amazing stone, which he said had fallen from the skies. This crystal, the farmer claimed, had the power to make a fir cone grow into a mighty pine tree in the blinking of an eye, thereby defying the rules of time.

Intrigued, the mathemagician turned his attention away from the four elements, and onto time itself.

He set to work, knowing that if he should succeed

in controlling the passage of time, he would become the most powerful man who ever lived. He knew too, that there were those – jealous of his power and influence – who would stop at nothing to prevent this from happening.

And so he swore Wytchwood to secrecy. No one should hear of his experiments. Not even the prince knew what the mathemagician had in mind.

Though Wytchwood did not tell a soul, he thought Magoria's plans were dangerous and unwise.

"Should you be working with something you do not fully understand, Master?" he asked.

But Magoria would have none of it. "My magic is strong enough to tame the most powerful of forces," he reasoned. "The people of Alpenpfalz live tough lives. It's their hard work which pays for the prince's fine life and, in turn, for my magical creations. Let us repay the debt we owe them by finding a way of bending the will of the crystal to relieve their misery."

Fine words, thought Wytchwood, but he suspected that his master's real motive was to prove himself the greatest sorcerer the world had ever known.

"I am going to build a clock tower – an ornate casing worthy of housing this crystal at its heart," Magoria explained. "But it will be no ordinary clock. This magical clock will enable me to control time, so the people's lengthy hours of toil will speed by in an instant, while their moments of happiness will seem to last for ever. It will be my Clock of Fortune."

"*Control* time?" Wytchwood protested. "Impossible. It can't be done! Time is but a measure of whether things are past, or present, or yet to come."

"How little you've learned, Wytchwood," the mathemagician scoffed. "How wrong you are. With this crystal and my strongest magic, I shall be able to make the past the present and the future the past – whatever I want. I will be able to speed time up and slow it down."

Still Wytchwood protested at the danger of working with the unknown. But the mathemagician would have none of it. "Enough!" he commanded. "*I* am the master and *you* the apprentice."

And all the while, the curious crystal pulsed and glowed in its lead box on the workbench beside them.

Despite Wytchwood's fears, the project got underway. Magoria drew up plans for a tower that would house the crystal, and began weaving the magic that would control it and, therefore, time itself.

Following his master's specifications to the smallest measurement, Wytchwood organized the construction of the tall, black tower in the mountainous forest near the royal palace. The work was carried out behind a huge magical screen, so that none of the townsfolk or villagers could see what was being built.

Six months after work had begun, Magoria let it be known that the Grand Opening Ceremony would soon take place. The local people were beside themselves with expectation, while the prince sent out gold-edged invitations to numerous neighbouring dignitaries he wished to impress with his mathemagician's latest wonder.

When the appointed day finally arrived, the population of Oberdorf had swelled to ten times its usual number. People had come from far and wide, from villages and towns and other kingdoms, to witness the unveiling of the mysterious object. In pride of place, at the very front of the crowd, sat the prince with his new bride.

Magoria stood before his creation. He looked up and raised his hands high. "I give you, the Clock of Fortune," he cried.

As the words echoed round the air, the magical screen, which for so long had thwarted the best efforts of the curious villagers to see through it, simply vanished into thin air.

The crowd gasped as one, as the magnificent clock tower was revealed, dwarfing the trees around it. It pointed towards the sky like a black marble finger.

Everybody crowded around to admire the intricate stonework of the spiral staircase. They wondered at the ornate carving of the tower, and were bedazzled by the beautiful clock faces. But what was it for? they asked one another. Where was the magic?

"What you see is merely the outer shell," the mighty mathemagician cried. "The true wonder lies within its heart, which shall control time at my bidding. Winters will be short, and summers long. Bad times will become a thing of the past. From this moment forth I shall see to it that only good times prevail."

"Thank you, thank you," cried the crowd and, as a cheer echoed around the trees, Magoria swept round, gown flapping, and placed the palm of his hand against a raised square of marble on the side of the tower. Everyone drew in their breath.

There was a moment of silence, and then sparks flew and the air crackled with the sound of magic. A look of confusion and horror passed over Magoria's face and he was thrown backward.

DONG! The bell tolled. It was deafeningly loud. The horses of the prince's carriage flattened their ears in panic and reared up on their hind legs. DONG! The people clung to one another in fear.

DONG!

Beneath this sound, another one was forming. Deep

and throaty, it sounded like a chuckle rising in the throat of some giant beast...

Something was wrong. That much was clear to everyone. No matter how many times Magoria pressed his hand to the marble, the Clock would not do his bidding.

"What is happening?" the prince called out.

The question was answered not by Magoria, but by a booming voice which came from within the clock itself.

"I AM HAPPENING," it roared. "FOR I CONTROL THE CYCLE OF THE SEASONS; THE TIMING OF THE TIDES; THE WAXING AND WANING OF THE MOON ABOVE AND THE MOVEMENT OF THE SUN..."

The clock was *speaking*. It had a voice. Surely even Magoria's greatest magic could not achieve such a thing? And what a voice it was, unlike any other heard upon this Earth. Terrifying yet hypnotic. The crowd hung upon its every word.

The mathemagician fell to his knees and hammered desperately on the side of the clock. "Stop it, stop it!" he cried – but in vain. The voice would not be stilled.

"PITIFUL FOOLS," it bellowed. "DID YOU REALLY HOPE TO CONTROL ME? FOR NOW I CONTROL TIME ITSELF, AND THUS THE GAMES WE PLAY."

"Magoria, explain yourself!" the prince shouted above the noise. "How does this machine come to *speak*? Explain!"

"THIS PUNY MAN DID NOT CREATE ME," the Clock continued. "HE IMPRISONED ME WITHIN THIS MARBLE TOMB, BUT HIS MAGIC AND MACHINERY HAVE MAGNIFIED MY POWERS. SPEECH IS BUT CHILD'S PLAY COMPARED TO WHAT ELSE I CAN DO..."

And as it spoke, an icy blizzard began to blow. It whistled through the trees and howled around the tower, covering everything in its path with a thick layer of pure white snow.

Magoria turned to the prince, his face ghostly pale. "Believe me, Your Highness," he cried out. "This is not what I intended."

"WHAT *YOU* INTENDED?" the Clock boomed. "IT IS WHAT *I* INTEND THAT MATTERS NOW."

The gathering of people cowered in fear, and rightly so, for this magical Clock with the crystal from the skies at its very heart, passed judgement on all those assembled there.

"YOU, MAGORIA," it began, "THE WORM WHO DARED TO HARNESS ME, WILL BE PUNISHED FOR YOUR INTERFERENCE IN MATTERS YOU DO NOT UNDERSTAND. FOR THIS, I CONDEMN YOU TO LIVE

FOR EVER AND EVER AND EVER..."

A gasp went up from the crowd. Living for ever was a punishment? Magoria raised his eyes in surprise. It seemed to him more like a reward.

"YOU, WYTCHWOOD," the clock went on in its unearthly tone, "SAW THE ERROR OF YOUR MASTER'S WAYS FROM THE BEGINNING. IF YOU LEAVE THE KINGDOM, NEVER TO RETURN, I SHALL SEE NO HARM BEFALLS YOU. BUT IF YOU, OR ANY OF YOUR KIN SET FOOT HERE AGAIN, YOU WILL SUFFER THE SAME FATE AS THE REST OF THOSE GATHERED HERE TODAY."

There was an eerie silence as the crowd waited to hear their own fate. They didn't have to wait long.

"HOW DARE ALL OF YOU THINK THAT *I* COULD BE CONTROLLED FOR *YOUR* PLEASURE. I BRING YOU THE GREATEST PUNISHMENT OF ALL – A WORLD WHERE TIME RUNS WILD, AT MY BIDDING. BUT WHEN WILL THIS FATE BEFALL YOU?" the Clock's voice bellowed. "MAYBE IN AN HOUR FROM NOW, MAYBE A WEEK, MAYBE A THOUSAND YEARS. YOU WILL LIVE EVERY WAKING MOMENT IN THE FEAR THAT IT COULD BE THE LAST BEFORE YOU FEEL MY WRATH... THE LAST BEFORE THE DAY OF DOOM ARRIVES." The voice roared, and the forest echoed with the cacophonous cackle of its hideous laughter.

As the Clock fell silent, a deathly hush descended over the forest. The next moment a man's voice cried out from the back of the crowd.

"What have you done to us, Magoria?"

"Why do you get to live for ever, whilst the rest of us live in fear?" shouted someone else.

"Our lives are ruined thanks to you!" yelled a third.

"The Clock of Fortune?" cried the prince himself. "What you've built is the Clock of Doom!"

And as the people shouted and bemoaned their fate, an extraordinary scene unfolded before them. The trees around the Clock of Doom began to grow. Creepers and vines snaked out of the ground as though they were live animals, and great bushes of thorns sprang out of nowhere. Was this a taste of what was to come?

By the time the terrified people had run down the mountainside, the clock tower was completely covered by the forest. Not even its uppermost tip could be seen above the trees.

When the prince reached the palace gates with his terrified bride, he watched in horror as the magnificent building aged a thousand years and crumbled away to dust.

As for wise Wytchwood, he fled the kingdom, never to return.

But what of Magoria the Mathemagician? He still lives. Even his strongest magic could not break the curse put upon him by the Clock of Doom. He is living out his sentence of a life without end, hidden in his secret chamber; and will be a hundred years hence, or even a thousand. For, remember, mankind is a slave to time, not time to mankind.

Chapter Nine
Trapped

Ryan closed the book and stared down at the cover. The gold letters announced:

LOCAL MYTHS & LEGENDS

He looked up to find Marta Martine staring at him intently. "Well?" she said.

Ryan shrugged. "It's just a story. A fairytale about a speaking clock," he said, trying to laugh it off. "The only speaking clock *I'm* ever likely to hear is over the telephone." He smiled again.

"Oh, is that all?" said the old woman, with a

pained expression on her extraordinary face. "You dream of a clock tower so clearly that you recognize it from the woodcut. The clock in your dream speaks which, you've just admitted, is an unusual occurrence... "

"Yes...well...er..." Suddenly an idea struck Ryan. "I can explain that," he said.

"How?"

"My dad comes from Oberdorf. He grew up here," said Ryan. "He must have told me the legend years ago. Then coming here has jogged my memory. Made me dream about it."

"And how can you explain the voice inside your head?"

"I don't know," Ryan admitted.

The old woman rose from her chair. "I gave up my career to devote my life to the study of folklore and legends of this forest, and I tell you, Ryan Schilling, the Clock of Doom is not just a tale, it exists."

"Okay," said Ryan, who'd had a thought. "So if this legend *is* true, the Clock's curse came to nothing. I don't see anyone living in fear of the Clock around here nowadays. Do you?"

"But people forget, Ryan. That's something the Clock didn't think of. It misjudged the length of people's memories," sighed Miss Martine. "Hundreds of years may be nothing to the Clock...but to us? That's many generations."

"So where is it then, this Clock?" said Ryan.

Marta Martine breathed in sharply and walked over to the window. "It's out there somewhere," she said. "Hidden among the trees where the forest is at its thickest. Waiting. I've spent years trying to find it."

"Surely someone would have come across it by now, " Ryan reasoned. "By accident, even."

"Perhaps the Clock of Doom didn't want to be found," said Miss Martine. "Until now."

Ryan twisted round to look at her. "What do you mean, 'until now'?" he asked nervously.

The old woman shrugged. Ryan felt it was time to leave. He couldn't wait to get away from the cramped wood cabin and its strange occupant.

He stood up. "I really must go," he said. "Thank you for the coffee..."

"No. Thank *you* for the coffee," said Marta Martine with a strange smile. "I didn't mean to frighten you with all this talk," she added. "But it's best to know what you might be walking into."

"Yes," said Ryan, doubtfully. "Thanks again."

"Forewarned is forearmed," she said.

At the front door, Ryan clipped the leash back

onto Max's collar, and the pair of them stepped out into the snow. He'd forgotten how bitterly cold it was outside.

"Take care," Marta Martine called out as they set off across the clearing. "Keep to the track, and make sure you don't stop until you get back home."

"I will," Ryan called.

"And come and visit me again when the weather improves!" she added.

Not in a million years, thought Ryan. Miss Marta Martine was completely batty!

As he and Max made their way down through the trees, the dog started to act strangely. Every so often, he would tug Ryan to one side or the other, then stop and bare his teeth at something – or somebody – in the undergrowth. And the silence all around... It was eerie. The snow deadened every sound.

Ryan looked nervously about him. "Are you sure this is the right way, Max?" he said.

Max responded by howling up into the gloom of the forest canopy. The next instant, he bounded forward – off the track and into the undergrowth – pulling Ryan with him. Ryan lurched forward and, as the huge dog ran on, he needed all his strength just to keep hold of the leash.

"Stop, Max!" he shouted breathlessly, as

branches and brambles scratched at his face and hands. "Heel!"

But the dog would not obey. It was as if he were responding to a stronger command, and there was nothing Ryan could do to stop him. "Please, Max, I can't go this fast!" he panted. Ryan's foot suddenly caught in a loop of gnarled root. He cried out in surprise as he found himself flying through the air. He landed on the icy ground with a heavy crash. As he did so, the dog leash was wrenched from his grasp, and Max darted off into the shadowy undergrowth.

"Come back Max!" Ryan shouted. But, finding himself free at last, the dog had wasted no time in getting as far away as possible. Ryan was alone in the forest.

Shaking, he struggled to his feet. He had to find a way out of the trees. I'll be all right, he thought, as long as I keep going downhill. That way, I'm bound to come to the village in the end.

This was a good theory, yet the further Ryan went, the more uncertain he became. Not only did he fail to come to a path, but the forest itself became denser than ever.

The trees were growing so close together that, now and then, Ryan had to squeeze sideways between their cold, rough trunks. He stumbled through the thick undergrowth. Pine needles slashed at his face, barbed thorns snagged his clothes and twisted roots tripped him...but on he went. Then suddenly he stopped in his tracks as a terrible thought struck him.

Wasn't this what had happened in his nightmare?

Suddenly, he began to imagine seeing those savage yellow eyes everywhere he looked. What if there really *were* wolves in the forest? His heart pounded. He was furnace-hot and glacier-cold at the same time. Sweat poured down his face and stung his eyes.

He started walking again, pushing on as quickly as he could. On and on he went. Time and again, the vicious thorns snagged his clothes and ropes of ivy barred his way, until finally – unable to go on and unable to go back – he found himself trapped in a wall of thorns.

Ryan peered around, helplessly. It was gloomy in the forest, and getting darker by the minute.

Twisting his arms back awkwardly, he managed to slip them out of the shoulder straps of his backpack and pulled the bag around in front of him. Then he loosened the drawstring and rummaged inside for the flashlight.

He pointed the beam of light up at the branches, down at the ground, into surrounding bushes. Dark wing-like shadows fluttered through the air like a flurry of bats. Ryan trembled.

"I've got to get out of here," he said out loud, deliberately breaking the oppressive silence.

He struggled with all his might to break through the dense, spiky undergrowth, but his gloves were torn off by thorns which scratched his stinging hands. He was *really* beginning to panic now.

He wished he had never left the house...

A thorny branch had ripped into the back of his padded jacket and no matter how hard he tried, Ryan could neither unhook himself nor take the jacket off.

If only he hadn't taken that not-so-urgent package to Marta Martine. If only Uncle Karl knew where he was. If only...

No one will ever find me here, he thought. At that moment, Ryan noticed something strange. For the most part, wherever he pointed the flashlight, the beam of light bounced off the tree trunks and away into the distance. But at one place, it was different. Just to his left, the beam seemed to hit some kind of shiny object which reflected the light right back into his eyes.

Cautiously, Ryan stretched out his arm and reached as far as the thorns and creepers would allow – fearful that, at any minute, a wolf might leap up and sink its fangs into his hand.

There was no wolf. Yet, when Ryan made contact with what was there, his blood turned to ice in his veins.

The object was cold, hard and smooth to the touch. He knew what it must be. It felt like the black marble clock tower of his nightmare. Had he really found the Clock of Doom?

Chapter Ten
Black Marble

Instinctively, Ryan tried to pull back. To his horror, he discovered he couldn't. Flat against the freezing cold stone, his hand had stuck fast. What was more, as he stood there – bent and shivering – Ryan realized that something even weirder was happening. The marble was beginning to vibrate.

What now? thought Ryan, tugging desperately at his hand. But he was still stuck. And all the while the vibrations were growing stronger.

No. It couldn't be happening... It was *impossible*... Okay, so there really was an old clock tower in the forest, but that didn't mean to say that any of the rest of the legend had to be true.

Suddenly, he remembered how the Clock of Doom had been activated in the story; how Magoria had *"placed the palm of his hand against a raised square of marble on the side of the tower"*. It had been the touch of the mathemagician's hand that had started up the Clock of Doom.

As he stood there, Ryan became aware of something else. There was a rumbling sound, and the black marble seemed to be getting warmer.

All at once, his hand broke free from the stone. Ryan rubbed his fingers. They were wet and tingly and throbbing with cold. But at least he was free.

Around him, the talon-like thorns had also unhooked themselves from his jacket. He could move again.

The next instant, Ryan's relief turned to disbelief, as he saw *how* he had been set free. A shiver of fear passed through him.

The creepers, climbers and thorny bushes were growing smaller. Ryan stared in utter amazement, as the vicious thorns retracted and the treacherous tendrils rewound, coiling their way into nothing.

Little by little, the forest floor was clearing itself of

all obstacles, in a curious process of growing-in-reverse.

Looking up, Ryan realized that, for the first time since Max had abandoned him, he could see the sky. Like the bushes on the ground, the branches of the massive pine trees overhead were shrinking. More than that, the trees themselves were growing smaller.

Ryan stood there as, little by little, the largest of the pines sank lower, while the smaller trees disappeared altogether. Completely dumbfounded, Ryan could only watch in silence as the forest slowly revealed what it had been guarding for hundreds and hundreds of years.

When the trees finally halted their mysterious vanishing act, Ryan found himself in a clearing. In front of him stood the clock tower, pointing towards the sky like a black marble finger.

This was the clock tower from his nightmare: the clock tower in the woodcut print hanging on the wall of the cottage in the woods. This was the black marble tower of the legend. He had found the Clock of Doom – or rather, the Clock of Doom had found him.

Now Ryan was really afraid. He felt sick. Sick with fear.

The forest clearing suddenly rang out with a tremendous cacophony of bells. Ryan clamped his hands over his ears and staggered back. Then, out of the chiming din, he heard the unearthly voice so familiar from his nightmare. Faint at first, it grew until it drowned out the sound of the bells themselves.

"YES, IT IS I," roared the voice. "THE ONE THEY CALL THE CLOCK OF DOOM."

Ryan shuddered. The extraordinary sonorous tone made him cower with fear.

He knew he had to think clearly. He must. There was a logical explanation for everything. There *had* to be. Didn't there?

He looked up at the tall black edifice. Its ornate decorations were as imposing as they were grotesque. High up above his head, a row of gargoyles grinned down at him maliciously.

Still looking up, Ryan walked slowly around the clock tower. Each of the four clock faces showed a different time. One o'clock, four o'clock, eight o'clock and twelve o'clock.

"TO THINK THAT FOOL MAGORIA BELIEVED HE COULD CONTROL ME," said the Clock, making Ryan jump. "WHAT FUN I'VE HAD WITH THE MEDDLESOME WRETCH! DO *YOU* KNOW WHO YOU ARE?" the Clock asked suddenly.

"Ryan Schilling," he muttered. Despite his fear, he felt faintly ridiculous speaking to an obelisk.

"YOU ARE THE FIRST DESCENDANT OF THE APPRENTICE, WYTCHWOOD, TO SET FOOT IN OBERDORF SINCE THE DAY HE FLED," the unearthly voice bellowed. "I SENSED YOUR ARRIVAL THE MOMENT YOU CROSSED THE BORDER. NOW THE TIME APPROACHES FOR YOU TO PAY THE PRICE FOR COMING TO THIS LAND—"

"I don't know what you're talking about!" said Ryan.

"—AND AT THE SAME TIME, I'LL METE OUT THE HAVOC THAT I PROMISED THE PATHETIC CREATURES OF THIS PLACE." Once again it cackled with laughter. "HOW I WILL ENJOY THEIR JOLLY LITTLE DANCE OF CHAOS!"

That was when Ryan made a decision – and the decision was not to stick around. Turning on his heels, he dashed off blindly into the forest. The Clock of Doom disappeared from view – but inside Ryan's head, its wicked laughter echoed louder than ever.

Chapter Eleven
Out of Time

On and on Ryan ran, dodging this way and that between the trees, hopping over the stepping stones across a thawing stream, skidding around boulders and bramble bushes. The snow was melting all around him, dripping from branches and turning to slush. It wasn't long before he was panting noisily. His breath billowed from his mouth, his blood pounded in his ears and – despite the cold – sweat poured down his face as he rushed headlong down the tree-covered mountainside.

Got to escape, he thought, over and over. Got to get away.

He came to a fallen tree trunk. Running too fast to stop, Ryan sprang off the slushy ground and flew over the obstacle. As he landed, his ankle went over and a searing stab of pain made him yelp in agony. But he couldn't stop. He couldn't rest for a second. He had to get away...

He came to a fallen tree trunk. Running too fast to stop, Ryan sprang off the slushy ground and flew over the obstacle. As he landed, his ankle went over and a searing stab of pain made him yelp in agony. But he couldn't stop. He couldn't rest for a second. He had to get away...

He came to a fallen tree trunk. *No!*

With supreme effort, Ryan managed to stop himself from springing over it. This wasn't right. It was the *third* time he'd come to the fallen tree trunk. Time was playing tricks on him. Had the threatened chaos already begun?

In an effort to break out of the time loop once and for all, he walked around the tree instead of going over it. Only when he was on the other side did he start running again.

Once more, he was racing over the bouncy mattress of pine needles. Dodging obstacles, leaping holes, slipping on patches of melting snow. Until suddenly, there they were! The lights of the village twinkling below him. At last! he thought.

He aimed the beam of his flashlight at his watch. 5:30:10. He should be back in about ten minutes. The thought gave Ryan his second wind, as he set off down the steep slope.

Farther and farther he ran, loping through the deep drifts. On and on and on. And yet, no matter how fast his legs moved, the twinkling lights never seemed to get any nearer. It was as if he was running on the spot. He glanced at his watch again.

"No-o!" he howled.

It still said 5:30. The light on the digital display was flashing on and off with the seconds, but the number itself did not change. 10, 10, 10, 10, it was blinking, over and over.

It was then that Ryan noticed the village clock chiming the half-hour below him. The sound was echoing endlessly, as if the Clock of Doom had frozen time itself.

Not knowing what else to do, Ryan started running again. He could only hope that the treacherous clock would finally tire of its games and let him go.

Suddenly, the lights disappeared. Ryan cheered! If something had changed, it meant that time was moving once more.

He ran on, trying to catch another glimpse of the town. All at once he stumbled and went over on his ankle again. He collapsed on the ground and rubbed the painfully throbbing joint. The next moment – not wishing to waste any time – he was up and off again at full pelt. Sweat pouring, blood pumping, he drove himself on, his breath filling the air like dragon's smoke.

He was slowly feeling more and more energetic; his tiredness disappeared. Around boulders and bramble bushes he ran, across the stepping stones of a thawing stream, through the trees, that way and this.

Yet as he ran, Ryan realized that, once again, something was wrong. His heart was hammering furiously, but not with exhaustion. It was with blind terror. Something had happened; or was about to happen. He stopped in his tracks and spun round. There, in front of him, was the Clock of Doom.

"HOW I WILL ENJOY THEIR JOLLY LITTLE DANCE OF CHAOS!" the terrible voice boomed.

Ryan trembled. Those were the last words the Clock had said to him. He was right back where he'd started. Time itself held him in its terrifying grip.

How was he ever going to break free?

Chapter Twelve
Magoria Speaks

Suddenly, something felt different. The atmosphere had changed. Although the sky was still dark, Ryan didn't feel threatened any more. As abruptly as the evil power of the Clock of Doom had started up, so it seemed to have vanished.

Ryan felt a flood of relief. "It's just a great slab of black marble," he muttered.

Ryan's head was suddenly filled with the sound of a voice. He gasped. It was the voice that had called to him when he was in Miss Martine's cabin.

"*I wish it were!*" it said.

Ryan froze. The hairs on the back of his neck

stood up in alarm.

"*I wish it were!*" the voice repeated. Someone, or something, was inside his mind.

"Who are you?" Ryan demanded.

"*I am the fool who brought the curse upon this place,*" said the voice, and gave a wheezy cough.

"What's happening to me?" Ryan shouted. "Am I going crazy?"

"*No, Ryan Schilling,*" said the voice. "*It's time you heard the truth. I am Magoria the Mathemagician.*"

Ryan laughed nervously. "Magoria? From the legend?"

"*Like the Clock of Doom and the tricks it plays with time, I am a reality,*" the voice told him, earnestly.

This couldn't be happening. It just couldn't be. "You'd be hundreds of years old," Ryan protested.

"*You know the legend, Ryan Schilling. I am condemned to live for ever and ever and ever. Once I was Magoria the Mathemagician, now Magoria the Moribund would be more accurate.*"

"Moribund?" said Ryan, chewing his lower lip nervously.

"*It means that I am dying, as we all are,*" Magoria explained in his quavering voice. "*Yet for me, death itself remains tantalizingly out of reach. I grow older and older and older, but cannot die. For that is what eternity*" *on Earth must be, Ryan – everlasting old age,"* he sighed, and Ryan heard the desperation in the old man's voice. *"I need you to help me destroy this...this monster that I have unleashed upon the world."*

"Me?" said Ryan.

"Yes, you," came the reply. *"Didn't you hear what the Clock told you? You are a descendant of the long-dead Wytchwood... Not a Wytchwood by name, but by blood, for there is Wytchwood blood in your mother's veins."* He paused for breath. *"It is your presence which caused the storm, the tear in the sky, the reappearance of the Clock itself...and which has caused it to choose this moment to wreak havoc on the people of this land."*

"How was I to know?" exclaimed Ryan. This was too much.

"Your ignorance is of no concern to the Clock of Doom," said Magoria sharply. *"What is important is this: it's up to you to stop the Clock before it is too late."*

"Stop it?" cried Ryan. "It's not like my alarm clock, you know. I can't just take out the batteries!"

"Be still, Ryan Schilling!" the voice commanded. *"And listen closely. I don't have much time. For now, the Clock is resting, recharging. If you fail, the tricks it has already played on you will seem like mere games."*

"But I—" Ryan began.

"A lifetime of joy will speed past in an instant,"

Magoria went on. *"A moment's pain will become an eternity of suffering. The Clock of Doom shall reign over chaos, confusion and destruction."*

"You created it," Ryan said angrily.

"No. Wytchwood was right, Ryan. What I created was the clock tower and a way of magnifying the power of the crystal – but the crystal itself was not of my making. It fell from the sky. It was from another place beyond our world. How foolish I was to think that I could control something which I could never fully understand. But I have paid the price for that terrible mistake, believe me," said Magoria.

Ryan remained silent.

"But if you will not help destroy it for my sake, Ryan, then think of the others in the village and the town below," Magoria reasoned. *"Think of your Uncle Karl and Aunt Ingrid. All will perish if you turn away."*

"Everyone except you," said Ryan.

"If you succeed, however," came Magoria's weary voice, *"the curse will be removed from the land and I will finally be released from this never-ending torment. Come and talk to me face to face, Ryan Schilling. Let us talk in person."*

"But where are you?" Ryan asked, reluctantly.

"Where I always am," Magoria groaned. *"Imprisoned in my secret chamber underneath the old royal hunting lodge."*

"Hunting lodge?" said Ryan. "Where's that?"

"*Long gone, I'm afraid...*"

"So what are you underneath now?" Ryan interrupted.

"*The ground*," the old man wheezed.

Ryan shuddered. "Then how will I find you?" he asked.

There was a pause. For a moment, Ryan thought the mathemagician had gone. Then he heard him speak. "*There is a way*," he said falteringly. "*The entrance to my underground chamber lies...*" The voice stopped.

"Magoria? Magoria?" Ryan called.

"*...lies where the Clock points at nine. Come as soon... as soon as you can, Ryan,*" said the sorcerer, his voice growing weaker still, "*so that we may put an end to the hideous curse of the Clock of Doom once and for all.*"

Ryan was confused. "Where the Clock points at nine?" he said. "What does that mean?"

But if he knew, then Magoria was no longer able to say. His voice had all but given up on him. "*No more,*" he whispered croakily, and faded away into nothing.

Chapter Thirteen

A Race Against Time

Cold and frightened, Ryan stood in the forest clearing, the clock tower looming up before him...trying to make sense of what Magoria had said.

Where the Clock points at nine. What did it mean? None of the hands on the clock tower showed nine o'clock, so that was no help. What should he do?

Ryan wasn't much good at puzzles, and that was what this was beginning to feel like. *Where the Clock points at nine.* It was a direction. It was supposed to be telling him where to go.

Clocks don't give directions, thought Ryan. But compasses do! He pulled out the compass from his backpack. It looked just like a clock face. North was straight ahead, where twelve o'clock should be. South was at six o'clock, east was at three o'clock...and west was at *nine* o'clock.

Trust an old sorcerer to speak in riddles. Why couldn't he have simply said, "go west"? Ryan wanted to check that he'd understood the instructions correctly but, though he called his name, Magoria's voice did not return.

Ryan set out westward, in a straight line from the clock tower. It was easy enough to keep on course in the newly created clearing, but harder once he entered the forest. He had to keep an eye on the compass as he weaved his way through the trees.

There was no sign of the remains of a building. In time, the forest began to thin and the snow on the ground grew thicker.

Then, as twilight turned to night, Ryan caught a glimpse of the moon through the treetops. He found himself thinking about Uncle Karl and Aunt Ingrid. They'd be worried sick about him, but he had more important things to think about right now.

It was getting colder. Ryan wrapped his coat tightly around him, and pulled his collar up against the icy wind.

The snow had frozen over. With each step he

took, Ryan's boots crunched through the thin crust.

He was tired and hungry, and the coldness ached in his bones. Above his head, an owl glided through the air on silent wings. Ryan looked down at the compass.

"No!" he gasped in horror. He was heading *due north*. How long had he been going in the wrong direction? When did he last check the compass?

"Where am I?" he cried. His voice echoed away, unanswered. He glanced at his watch. By a cruel twist of fate, it was actually nine o'clock.

Ryan had never felt more alone in his life...and he knew he could never survive a night in the forest.

Lifting his head wearily, he pointed the flashlight up ahead. At first, he couldn't believe his eyes. He loped forward a few paces and looked again. Yes! There was something there. It looked like a chimney.

Suddenly, with a last burst of energy, Ryan struggled down the snowy hillside at the edge of the forest. A roof came into view, and then log walls with small windows. The next minute he found himself standing in front of a log cabin. He may not have found the remains of the old hunting lodge, but at least he'd found shelter.

Ryan clomped up the stairs, across the veranda, and knocked at the door. There was no answer. He knocked again and put his ear against the wood to listen. Still nothing.

With his heart in his mouth, he lifted the latch and pushed. The door was not locked.

"Hello?" Ryan called out into the darkness.

There was no answer. He walked inside, shut the door behind him and lit up the empty room with his flashlight. Slipping off his backpack, he slumped to the floor exhausted.

Ryan woke with a start as the bright, early-morning sunlight streamed into the room. He sat up, wondering for a moment where he was. Then he remembered.

He couldn't believe that he'd actually fallen asleep. Then a creeping fear entered his thoughts. Had the Clock of Doom been playing tricks with time again? Just how long *had* he been sleeping? He had to get a move on...but pangs of hunger made him think of food. He was starving.

Searching some cupboards, he found a few stale crackers and some jam, which he spread on them with a finger. He washed down his "meal" with a mouthful of snow.

Then Ryan stepped out again onto the veranda. The sun was still low in the sky, and he had to shield his eyes as he surveyed the icy winter scene.

He saw his footprints leading back up the hill. He saw the forest in the distance – and could clearly see the sinister Clock of Doom, standing tall above the trees, silhouetted against the sky. It was casting a long, thin shadow, which fingered its way across the snow-covered land.

"Of course!" Ryan exclaimed, and shook his head. "I've been such an idiot."

If Magoria had wanted him to go west, he'd have said so. But he hadn't. *"The entrance to my underground chambers lies where the Clock points at nine."*

Quite simply, Magoria had meant the direction of the shadow cast by the tower when the sun hits it at nine o'clock.

Ryan squinted back across the slopes. From where he was standing he could not see where the shadow came to an end – but he knew it was a long way off. If he was right, at nine o'clock precisely it would be pointing at the entrance to Magoria's underground chamber. Of course! The old wizard must have meant nine in the *morning* – there'd be no shadow in the dark! He checked his watch.

There's still time, thought Ryan, with a fresh surge of hope. I still have a chance, so long as I don't blow it. He hurried back inside for his backpack.

At eight o'clock on the dot, he set out into the thick, treacherous snow. He had exactly one hour to reach the end of the shadow.

Slipping, sliding, stumbling; every step was a nightmare. Time and again, he looked up at the Clock of Doom, black against the sun; time and again, he checked its dark shadow. Yet no matter how far he went, it never seemed to come any closer.

I'll never make it, Ryan thought. No. I've *got* to make it! But what if the Clock plays around with time again? Don't think about it, he told himself. Just keep moving.

With his lungs aching and his heart pounding fit to burst, Ryan tramped on as fast as he could. Valuable seconds passed, minutes passed. Time was ticking away...

Only ten minutes to go... Suddenly, without any warning, the ground disappeared in front of him. Ryan lost his footing and rolled, head over heels, down a steep bank – and onto a track.

He picked himself up. On he ran until, there in front of him, a thick black line lay across his path. The next moment, he was standing in the middle of the shadow of the Clock of Doom itself.

Would the Clock react to his being there? Would

it stop Ryan from reaching the spot where the shadow pointed? There was only one way to find out.

He scrabbled up the bank and glanced at his watch again. Time had almost run out. Trying hard to keep to the firmer snow, Ryan picked his way along the length of the dark shadow, towards its tip.

He reached the end with moments to spare. At nine o'clock precisely, the tip of the clock tower's shadow touched a half-concealed rock directly in front of him.

Slowly, anxiously, Ryan pulled away piles of dead branches from the rock. It turned out to be part of a stone wall. He looked behind it and found himself staring into the shadows of a deep hole. He directed his flashlight into the darkness. Stone stairs led down under the ground.

"Yes!" he shrieked, and his triumphant cry echoed through the forest.

Chapter Fourteen

Going Underground

Swiping at thick nets of dusty cobwebs, Ryan began the long descent down the shadowy staircase. At the bottom, he found himself in a narrow stone corridor. He walked along it, shivering nervously in the cold, dank air. At the end, he came to a door.

Grasping the heavy iron handle, Ryan turned it and put his shoulder to the solid wood. The rusty hinges creaked as the door swung open. Ryan cautiously slipped in and waved his flashlight around.

He groaned. Surely this wasn't Magoria's secret chamber at all? It looked like a wine cellar – a huge wine cellar, with a vaulted ceiling, thick pillars and row upon row of gigantic wooden barrels lying on their sides, like rows of gypsy caravans.

There was no sign of Magoria, but something told Ryan that only a prince would have such a grand cellar, which meant that this had to be the royal hunting lodge. So where *was* Magoria?

"Magoria," he called out. His voice echoed around the empty vault and faded away, unanswered. He called again. Still nothing.

Ryan shone his flashlight around the cellar. The ancient sorcerer had to be in here somewhere. As the beam of light fanned out onto the huge casks, something glinted from each of them. Ryan went to take a closer look at one of the barrels.

There, screwed to the round upturned end of the wine barrel, was a brass plate with a name and number on it.

"*Hallenfeld: 118*," Ryan read out loud, and shrugged. The name meant nothing to him. Walking further on, he spotted a name that seemed more familiar: *Waldburg*, followed shortly after by *Steinfeld*. Of course, these were the names of the places he'd passed on the journey to Oberdorf.

But the name on the next barrel was new to him. It read: *Hexenmeisterbräu*. Ryan grinned.

"Wizard's brew," he translated. Beneath the name, instead of a number, there was a looping symbol that looked like a long, flattened figure eight lying on its side.

This was the symbol scientists used for *infinity*. For ever and ever and ever – just like the punishment given to the mathemagician. Very clever, thought Ryan. Was this his hiding place?

"Magoria!" he shouted, and hammered on the end of the barrel with his fist. "Are you in there?"

Ryan pointed the beam of his flashlight at the front edge of the barrel. If this was the right place, then there should be...a pair of hinges, which meant that on the *opposite* edge... "Yes!" said Ryan as his feverish fumblings were rewarded.

There was a loud "click" as a catch unlocked, and the circular front of the barrel swung open. Ryan found himself staring into a gaping black hole.

"Magoria?" he repeated, more quietly this time. Silence.

For a moment, Ryan hesitated. What next? Come on, he thought, as he stepped onto the rim. I can't back out now.

He crept inside the empty barrel and took a couple of nervous paces forward...then a few more, and a few more.

The round door behind him slammed shut with a tremendous *bang*.

Ryan jumped. The flashlight slipped from his hand and crashed to the floor. The light went out. He was trapped.

Chapter Fifteen
From Bad to Worse

Ryan stood inside the pitch-black barrel. This was no secret chamber. What if the whole thing had been a trap? "Magoria!" he yelled. Again, there was no reply.

Wobbly and awkward on the curved floor, it was all Ryan could do to remain upright.

Suddenly, from behind him, Ryan heard a sound that turned his stomach and made his flesh crawl... It was the sound of tiny claws scratching at the wood. *Rats*.

His mind was filled with images of twitchy pink noses, sharp claws and vicious yellow teeth.

There it was again: *scratch, scratch, scratch,*

followed by a high-pitched shriek echoing around and around the barrel. To his horror, Ryan realized that it was *him*! He was screaming.

The next instant, a crack of light appeared at the far end. Ryan held his breath.

A door was opening and then, silhouetted against a green glow beyond, he could see a tall, long-haired figure in a flowing dark robe.

Ryan stepped forward, wincing at the harsh light. "Magoria?" he said uncertainly. The figure before him wasn't at all what he'd expected. It was much younger.

"Indeed, I am," the man replied. Ryan paused. The voice was no longer old and frail. "Come in, Ryan Schilling," said the man, beckoning impatiently.

The underground chamber took Ryan's breath away. Flaming torches burned brightly in every nook and cranny. The walls were lined with long, heavy wooden tables, each one covered with the instruments of the sorcerer's craft – a huge brass model of the planets rotating around the sun, a pendulum clock and several weird-looking machines.

There were bottles and pots, all marked with neat labels. There were bundles of herbs and sacks of spices. A cauldron bubbled over a low fire, sending out wisps of steam.

At the far end, in an alcove in the stonework, a single flame flickered. It burned a deep emerald green that glowed on the surrounding rock.

Then something horrible happened. Magoria – the one who had greeted Ryan, with his smooth young face, long dark hair and fine robes – disappeared. In his place, stood a hideous figure of incredible age, with no hair, no teeth, and dressed in rags.

"What's happening?" Ryan gasped.

The ancient being raised his head, and turned one of his milky-grey eyes to look at him. A gnarled and scaly hand pointed at Ryan.

"Don't be afraid, Ryan... I have so little energy," the horrifying vision wheezed.

Suddenly – as if superimposed over the time-ravaged figure – the younger man reappeared. "So little energy left..." he rasped, before changing back again.

All at once, Magoria breathed in sharply. The proud features and upright figure returned, and remained.

"Now you know what eternal life can bring," he said. "I did not intend you to see me as I really am, but... Oh, I am weary, my boy. So weary. And all this shape projection only makes me all the wearier."

"Shape projection?" said Ryan.

Magoria smiled weakly. "I wanted to look my best when you arrived," he said. "So I conjured up the image of how I once looked. Alas, it is – as you now know – a mere illusion."

"But how?" said Ryan.

"There are many things I have taught my mind to do over the years," he explained. "As my body has grown frail, so I have developed my brain – with the aid of my sorcery, of course. How else do you imagine I knew you had returned? How else do you think I managed to talk to you inside your head and also read your thoughts? But enough of this idle chatter. There is so much we have to do if we are to put an end to the wicked curse of the Clock of Doom."

"You mean, so much *I* have to do," Ryan muttered.

Magoria looked at him sharply. "You're not thinking of giving up, are you? Can you imagine what it would be like if the Clock allowed time to run wild? Past, present and future would no longer have any meaning. Butterflies would crawl into empty cocoons and turn into caterpillars. Mountains would rise and fall in the twinkling of an eye. People would die before they had even been born... This must *never* be allowed to happen."

Ryan, who had been staring at Magoria, open-mouthed, finally found his voice. "But what on earth do you expect *me* to do?" he blurted out.

"Hush, Ryan Schilling, descendant of my wise apprentice," said the mathemagician, gently. "With a clear head and a valiant heart, you will succeed. But you must listen to me. And listen to me well. Make one mistake, and you will surely perish."

Chapter Sixteen

The Crystal Heart

With Ryan looking on, Magoria busied himself around the secret chamber. First he went to a desk and removed a yellowed scroll tied with a dusty red ribbon, and tucked it under his arm. Then he crossed to a tall bookcase, selected a large leather-bound book from the top shelf and pulled it out with a long, crooked finger.

"Oh," he gasped, as the heavy book slipped from his hand and fell to the floor. He stooped down and tried in vain to pick it up. "It's no good," he rasped. "I can't..."

Ryan hurried across the room, picked up the

book and held it out to Magoria. "Thank you, my boy," he said. "I'd be grateful if you could carry the book to the table for me." He smiled weakly.

As Ryan did as he was asked, it occurred to him just how weak Magoria's body must have become. The book wasn't heavy at all. He looked back at the mathemagician, standing tall and proud in his robes.

"A mere illusion," Magoria reminded him sadly.

Ryan nodded. The image of the ancient hideous creature the sorcerer had become was still clear in his mind.

"Not a pretty sight, eh?" Magoria sighed.

Ryan turned away, embarrassed. He had forgotten that Magoria was able to read his thoughts. "I'm sorry," he mumbled.

But Magoria brushed aside his apology with a wave of his hand. "Come now," he said. "You must be prepared for every eventuality. Open the book and find me the section entitled '*The Crystal Heart*'."

As Ryan flicked through the book, he saw page after page filled with countless spells and detailed diagrams involving air, earth, fire and water.

"Keep going," said Magoria, impatiently. "It's much further on."

Ryan went to the end of the book, and began turning the pages from the back. There were more spells, and still more diagrams of planets and constellations, of curious machines criss-crossed with arrows and annotations...and of the Clock of Doom itself.

Finally he came to the part Magoria had requested. In the middle of a page full of numbers and symbols was a drawing of the crystal heart.

"This," said Magoria, "is what gives the Clock its incredible powers. This is the crystal around which I constructed the whole clock tower. This is the heart which holds the power and makes everything possible..."

Ryan stared at the picture.

"Once you have entered the tower, Ryan, you must locate the crystal and destroy it. When you have done that, the Clock of Doom will be no more than..." he sighed, "...an over-sized ornament."

"That simple, eh?" said Ryan. "Are you trying to tell me that the crystal won't mind me smashing it to smithereens?"

"The crystal on its own has power, but not nearly the power it has as a part of the Clock," Magoria said, quietly. "My magic gave it strength."

"How?" asked Ryan.

"Its position in the tower, the siting of the tower itself. All these things have significance. When you weave a spell, the smallest detail is of the utmost importance."

"Okay, so it's not so strong on its own – but I still have to get into the tower in the first place," Ryan protested.

Ignoring him, Magoria went on. "The crystal is set in a marble slab in the middle of the uppermost chamber," he said. "The rounded end sticks out above the surface. You must seize it and pull it out of its setting. But beware that your fingers do not slip. You may not have more than one opportunity to remove the crystal. Do you understand?"

Ryan nodded nervously.

"When you have removed the crystal, take care not to look at it, for it will hypnotize you with its brilliance. Instead, you must destroy it. No one else must ever be tempted into thinking that they might be able to control it."

Destroy it! It sounded simple; too simple. Ryan's head spun. It was all down to him now, yet how he wished that Magoria might destroy the crystal on his own...

"I am too frail," Magoria said softly. "You know that."

"Not hundreds of years ago, you weren't," said Ryan.

Magoria sighed. "True," he said. "But the Clock has been dormant for many centuries – like a sleeping volcano – until you set foot in the land. Only now that it is active again can it be entered."

Typical, thought Ryan. It had to wait for *me* to come along. "But if it knows what I'm planning to do, surely it'll try to stop me?" he argued.

Magoria nodded. "It probably will," he agreed. "But I am here. I may be weak, but I still understand the magic of the Clock better than anyone else. I will do all I can to help you. And your greatest help is that the passage through the Clock to the crystal is an out-of-time corridor that I created."

"A what?" asked Ryan.

"I can't explain that now. There's too little time," Magoria snapped. "But while you are in this corridor, the powers of the Clock cannot affect you. Once you reach the chamber with the crystal, however, it will be a different matter."

Magoria pulled open a drawer in the heavy wooden table and started to rummage around. After a few moments he held up a scroll of parchment, sealed with red wax. He stared at it, lost in his own thoughts and recollections.

"So I go through this passage," said Ryan finally. "What next?"

"Next?" said Magoria. "Ah, yes. The ripples! The ripples!" He proceeded to break the seal of the scroll and unroll it across the table. "*The Ripples of Time*" it said across the top.

Ryan looked at it. It was a chart, like one of those diagrams showing the orbits of the planets. Around a bright circle in the middle were seven concentric circles, in all the colours of the rainbow.

"What are they?" asked Ryan.

"As it pulsates," Magoria explained, "the crystal sends out ripples, red or orange...all the way to violet. Each ripple is a different aspect of time – past, present, future... All you need to remember is that green is the present."

"So the others are—?"

"Dangerous? Oh yes," nodded the centuries-old sorcerer, reading Ryan's thoughts again. "Wait in the out-of-time corridor until the green ripple appears. When it is shining, you must go to the marble plinth and remove the crystal. But beware. You will have only fifteen seconds to do this. If you take any longer, the ripple will change from green and your body will pass into the past or the future."

"Which?" said Ryan.

"Who knows?" Magoria confessed. "Green may be followed by yellow or blue...it may hurl you into the future or thrust you into the past...the sequence is random."

"Oh," Ryan said quietly. "Just one more question. How do I actually get *into* the clock tower? How do I reach this out-of-time corridor?"

Magoria fell silent once more. Staring into midair, his face grew troubled. He scratched his head. He rubbed his chin. All at once, the face of the hideous, ancient Magoria reappeared, old beyond imagination, with his eyes of marble and his parchment skin. Then, as Ryan continued to stare in horror, the mathemagician began to fade completely.

"Magoria!" Ryan shouted. "How do I get inside the Clock of Doom? MAGORIA!"

The fast-fading shadow turned his head stiffly. "Inside?" he croaked.

"Yes, inside!" Ryan said, desperately. "Magoria, answer me."

For a moment, it seemed as though the ancient mathemagician was about to disappear completely. Ryan leaped forward and seized him by his shoulders.

Instantly, the figure became solid again, though still hideous.

"I must rest," he rasped wearily, and slumped to the floor. "You must press the smallest square on the upper parapet at one of the appointed times." His voice trailed away.

"The appointed times," said Ryan. "*What* appointed times?"

Magoria sighed, and coughed weakly. "The times on the faces of the clock," he said. "But...I do not remember what they are."

"But *I* do," said Ryan, with relief. "One o'clock, four o'clock, eight o'clock and twelve o'clock."

"That's it!" Magoria exclaimed, suddenly resuming his youthful appearance. "Well done, my boy! You are a credit to your ancestor, Wytchwood. It is time for you to go."

Ryan knew what he had to do, and he was afraid. Faced with the prospect of entering the Clock, he felt paralysed with fear.

"Farewell," said Magoria. "And... Oh!"

Ryan spun around. "What?" he said.

"A little thing I've just remembered," said Magoria, smiling sheepishly. "At the end of the out-of-time corridor is a sprung door – one that springs shut and locks when entered. It was designed for unwelcome meddlers. Even if they can get in, they certainly can't get out. Far simpler than a spell."

Ryan remembered his terror of being trapped

inside the stone coffin in his nightmare. "A *little* thing!" he exclaimed.

"It's all right," Magoria assured him, and pulled a key out from the folds of his gown. "This will let you out again."

"You're sure it'll work?" said Ryan.

"Of...of...of course, I'm..." Magoria stuttered and, once again, the upright figure of the mathemagician was replaced by his true hairless, toothless self. "It's no use," he croaked. "I cannot keep this up." He tossed the key to the floor.

"Take it and go!" he cried, and a bony yellow arm pointed to a low door in the far corner of the chamber. "It should lead you up to the surface. Farewell," he whispered. "And remember this, Ryan Schilling: you must not fail!"

Chapter Seventeen

Every second counts

Ryan finally emerged from the ground into the middle of some bushes. There was nothing to suggest that a building had once stood there.

He pushed the key that Magoria had given him into his pocket, and looked around. Far in the distance, the massive black tower stood high above the trees. He could only hope that there were no more "little things" that Magoria had forgotten to mention.

He set off. Over fields, through some woods, and back into the forest... Suddenly he realized he was not alone. In the distance were hordes of people

– men, women and children – approaching the clock tower. He headed towards them.

It was horrible. The *everydayness* of it appalled Ryan. These people were flocking to look at something more dangerous than the deadliest of weapons, and they were laughing and joking about it. Didn't they realize it was evil?

Of course not. How could they?

He wanted to scream out to them. He wanted to warn them what might happen. But they'd never believe him...and anyway he had no real idea of *what* exactly might happen if time ran wild.

"Wow," said a girl, looking at the clock tower up ahead. She pushed past him. "What an amazing-looking thing."

"What is it? I mean, who built it?" said her friend. "And how did they do it so quickly?"

The closer Ryan got to the tower, the thicker the crowd got. More and more people were streaming up the mountain towards the curious obelisk, which had so mysteriously appeared in the middle of the forest.

Then Ryan noticed that the air was growing warmer – and unusually quickly. Heavy loads of melting snow slipped down from the branches of the trees above, the earth turned to mud, and the forest floor was soon awash with widening streams of melting snow. Everything was happening so fast. Was the Clock already playing games?

At last, puffing and panting, Ryan emerged into the clearing directly in front of the Clock of Doom.

The whole area was thronging with excited people, all jostling for position and craning their necks for a better view. He checked his watch. It was five to one. Five minutes to go before the first of the appointed times.

Ryan pushed his way purposefully through the spellbound crowd. As he squeezed between two women right at the front, he groaned.

A rope had been put up, cordoning off the area around the tower. On the other side stood a fat, green-uniformed policeman with an even fatter police dog by his side.

Ryan groaned again. He had to get in there. But how?

The people around him were chattering excitedly, completely unaware of the horrors which would soon be unleashed if *he*, a descendant of Wytchwood, could not destroy the crystal in time.

Darting quickly under the rope, Ryan ran at the policeman and his dog, shouting and waving his arms wildly.

The dog barked and lunged at him. "Stay, boy!"

shouted the policeman. But, having been sitting still all morning, the dog was not about to miss out on the chance of some fun. As Ryan sped off around the back of the clock tower, the police dog wagged its tail and gave chase, dragging its hapless handler behind it.

Ryan glanced back as he rounded the last corner. Neither dog nor policeman were in sight. In front of him was the foot of the staircase which ran up the outside of the tower like a helter skelter. He raced for it and – egged on by the cheering crowd who thought it was all just a bit of harmless fun – bounded up the stairs, two at a time.

One flight, two flights... Six flights, seven flights... And up to the parapet. He looked at his watch again. Fifteen seconds to one o'clock... He searched anxiously for *the smallest square on the upper parapet.* And there it was – waist-high and a little to the right. The countdown began.

"Ten," he said. "Nine. Eight..."

At that moment, a heavy hand grabbed his shoulder and pulled him back. Ryan turned. It was the policeman, red-faced, sweaty and looking far from happy.

"What do you mean by breaking through the cordon?" he demanded.

"I'm sorry," Ryan said in his best German,

reaching behind his back with his right arm and placing his fingers gingerly against the square. "I... errm. That is... It was for a bet," he said.

"A bet?" the policeman wheezed. "You get me chasing all the way up here... This structure could be dangerous. And look at me and not your watch when I'm talking to you."

Three. Two. One... Push!

Ryan pressed the square in the stone as hard as he could. The door in the marble slid open, and Ryan tumbled inside.

"Here, what's going o—" he heard the policeman saying.

BANG! The door slammed shut. At last, Ryan had made it. He was inside the Clock.

Looking around, he realized at once how familiar it all was. The touch of the cold marble, the ornate carving of the bannister, the narrow slits in the wall which let in light. He was living his nightmare.

But there was no time to think about that now. He must concentrate on the task that lay ahead.

Ryan made his way up the spiral staircase. Suddenly, he heard something that made him stop dead. A low pulsing hum was coming from the crystal, like a giant heartbeat.

With his own heart pounding, Ryan raced up to

the top of the tower. Abruptly, the steps ended. In front of him was an arched doorway, and beyond that a passage. This was the out-of-time corridor. Ryan took a step forward.

The humming of the Clock stopped immediately. Ryan shuddered. There was absolute silence. Of course, having stepped out of time, he was listening to the sound of *nothing*.

Chapter Eighteen
The Dance of Chaos

He began to climb the steeply sloping passageway. Pale light streamed in through lancet windows which lined the outer wall. Pausing for a second to see what was going on outside, Ryan glanced out through one of the narrow openings.

What he saw made his stomach churn. He hurried to another window, and yet another. Each time, he was greeted with a similar sight. Down below him, the unsuspecting sightseers were moving around jerkily and at high speed. Watching them was like watching a scene from a film being fast-forwarded. Then, abruptly, the movement changed, and everyone started moving in reverse.

Back and forth. Fast, slow. Fast, slow. They were seized by a time loop and spun round and round... It looked to Ryan like some weird and frightening dance. Was this the dance of chaos the Clock had threatened in the legend?

The strange effect was made all the more weird by a flashing light. On, off, on, off, it went; faster and faster. It was as if a strobe light was flashing – making the people's movements look oddly graceful as they continued to move.

Ryan looked up at the sky. The reason for the curious light show was at once clear. Night was following day at a furious rate. Time and again the bright blue sky was torn away – like a page from a calendar – to reveal the blackness of night. It reminded him of when he had seen the rent in the sky on his first morning in Oberdorf.

But it was the look on the people's faces that made Ryan really shudder. They were creased with pain and fear.

"*A moment's pain will become an eternity of suffering,*" was how Magoria had described their punishment. And that was exactly how it looked.

I've got to stop all this, Ryan thought, turning and hurrying along the out-of-time corridor. I must destroy the crystal. The chamber was ahead of him now. It was bathed in a deep green light.

Ryan bounded forward, but the light turned to blue and he had to stop himself from hurtling into the chamber. His heart was pounding. That was close! He might have lost himself in another time and ended up unable to stop the chaos outside. He would have to wait until the green light returned.

He looked back out of the nearest window. As the nights and days continued to flash on and off, Ryan noticed that the people were getting younger. One old man threw away his walking stick and his hair turned from white to brown... He went from being stooped to upright, then shrank before Ryan's eyes until he was a baby.

One by one, *everyone* became a baby and vanished, until the clearing was totally empty. Ryan ran to the window on the other side of the corridor. Whichever way he looked, the view was the same. The people had all gone, banished to a time before they had even been born.

Ryan couldn't tear his gaze away from the terrible sight. No! thought Ryan. This can't be happening. It can't be. What could have happened to Uncle Karl and Aunt Ingrid?

Suddenly, out of nowhere, the ground was

covered in crying babies. They began to grow at different speeds, sprouting hair and getting bigger, growing up to become the people they had been before.

But it didn't stop there. Time was still moving forward at high speed.

Ryan realized to his horror that he'd been so engrossed in what was happening outside that he had missed a second opportunity to step through a safe, green ripple and seize the crystal. Outside, the people were getting older still.

Idiot! he thought. Now look what I've done!

Below him, the children were racing headlong towards old age, while old people simply keeled over, one by one. Within seconds, the clearing looked like a battlefield. It was strewn with bodies, which turned to skeletons, and then to dust, which blew away on the wind.

Ryan stared in horror.

He was too late.

He had failed.

The crowd, Uncle Karl, Aunt Ingrid, Max – maybe *all* the people in Oberdorf and even Steinfeld – were dead. The Clock of Doom had killed them all.

But no. Suddenly, the onlookers were back. This time, marching up the hill, as they must have done earlier that day. As Ryan kept watching, more and more people threaded their way up between the trees and stood, staring up at the clock tower.

"Go away!" he screamed. "It's dangerous here!" But no one could hear him. They were doomed to relive their fatal encounter with the Clock as many times as the Clock of Doom decreed.

A police van arrived, the rope cordon was put into place, and Ryan caught sight of the fat policeman and his dog taking up their positions at the bottom of the staircase. Suddenly, he saw someone else. A boy. He watched in mounting terror as the boy ducked under the rope and began leaping around like a maniac. "It's me!" he gasped, and the memory of his "living" reflection in his nightmare came flooding back to him.

Time had gone haywire. Already, the *other* Ryan was racing up the outside of the tower. Soon, he would come hurrying up the stairs.

Which is the real me? he wondered. Is that person any less *me* than I am? And what will happen if I meet myself? He didn't want to wait to find out.

He had to get into the chamber. He had to stop this madness. He tore back along the corridor, and was halfway through the door when he realized the ripple of light gleaming from the crystal was yellow, not green.

He pulled back at once. But it was already too late. The front of his body, which had been bathed in the warm, golden light, had dramatically aged.

His arms felt weak. There were brown spots of age on the back of his hands. He touched his face lightly with his fingers and recoiled at the touch of unfamiliar skin. It felt leathery, lined, more like the skin of a reptile than a human being.

"Oh, no," gasped Ryan, his voice strangely deep and old. "What have I done?"

Behind him, he caught a glimpse of a figure at the far end of the corridor. It was himself. He stared back into the yellow chamber. How would the sequence continue?

If it was green, he would be able to remove the pulsing crystal once and for all. If it was something else...he might age so much he'd die.

Behind him, his double moved closer – it was about to step into the out-of-time corridor. Ryan knew he had no choice but to step into the chamber. He closed his eyes: he stepped forward.

The stone door slammed shut behind him.

Chapter Nineteen

Ripples of Time

Ryan opened his eyes. There were no windows in the chamber; the only light came from the crystal itself. From the middle of a black marble plinth, at the heart of the room, it pulsed, a deep emerald green.

Ryan felt a flood of relief. He had been lucky...

"*Indeed,*" came the voice of Magoria in his head as he hurried across the chamber. "*Quickly, now. Remove the crystal while the Clock is still distracted and is wreaking havoc.*"

Ryan stretched across the marble plinth and looked down into the dome of the crystal bathed in green light. He found himself staring down at a night sky, studded with twinkling stars – a miniature universe.

He wondered where this incredible stone had originally come from. How many millions of miles had it travelled before falling to Earth? It was so beautiful...so very beautiful...like a giant emerald.

"Don't look into the crystal," Magoria's furious voice exploded in his head. *"Your fifteen seconds are almost up, then the light will change from green to—"*

Ryan placed his hands on the crystal, clasped the smooth surface, tugged – and slipped.

The yellow light had left his fingers old and weak. "No," he gasped.

He tried again, and again; the aged fingers lost their grip. The last remaining seconds were slipping quickly away...

"BACK AND FORTH AND BACK AGAIN," the Clock of Doom was bellowing outside. "EVERSOFAST... EV-ER SO SLO-W-W-W-W."

Ryan's head pounded with anxiety. "Come out!" he muttered through gritted teeth.

"AROUND AND AROUND AND AROUND YOU GO," bellowed the Clock of Doom.

"Yes!" Ryan cried. At last, painfully, he was managing to pull the crystal from the marble.

As it emerged from the hole, the crystal glittered

brilliantly and, as blue light pulsated, it looked like a giant sapphire.

"*Blue* light!" Ryan gasped. "Oh no!"

The ripples of time had already changed from green to blue. Straightening up sharply, Ryan yanked the crystal from its setting and raised it above his head. Then, with all the strength he could muster, he hurled the crystal down.

"NOOOOOOOOOOOO!!" screamed a voice, silenced in the second that the crystal crashed noisily against the stone floor. It exploded into a million pieces, which glowed for a moment longer, and then faded away.

"YES!" Ryan cheered into the sudden darkness.

He'd done it! He'd smashed the crystal and destroyed the Clock of Doom.

Or had he? Where was the door? Where was the keyhole?

He looked around blindly.

If he couldn't find it, then he'd be trapped. There would be no escape. Four cold, marble walls surrounded him. *No escape*. He was trapped inside the marble coffin of his nightmare.

Chapter Twenty

Full Circle

Ryan slumped down to the floor. "Magoria!" he called. "Magoria?" Nothing. Where was the reassuring voice inside his head? Ryan had shattered the crystal. He'd broken the curse...but had he also destroyed the mathemagician? Who would help him now?

Then something began to glow in front of him. At first, he thought it was just his eyes playing tricks but, as he concentrated on the dull light, it began to shine more brightly.

Terrified that it might disappear before he reached it, Ryan hurried back across the chamber, not even daring to blink. As he got closer, he saw that the light was spilling out from some kind of hole in the wall... It was a KEYHOLE!

"Yes!" Ryan shouted, ecstatically. He pulled out the key Magoria had given him, slid it into the lock and turned it. There was a soft click and the door sprang open. Ryan hurtled down the corridor.

As he ran, he noticed that his arms and hands were back to normal. How come? The blue light, he thought. This must have something to do with the blue light.

"*Exactly*," said Magoria's voice, deep inside his head. "*The blue ripple of time.*"

"You're still alive," said Ryan, quietly.

"*But fading fast, thanks to you, Ryan Schilling,*" said the weakening voice.

"Did the blue light undo the effects of the yellow light?" asked Ryan, trying to make sense of it all.

"*The yellow ripple aged you, and the blue ripple made you young again...*" Magoria wheezed.

"And yellow and blue make green..." said Ryan triumphantly, "...which is the present!"

"*Yes. You are as you were when you entered the clock tower. Now press the stone and leave once more. Goodbye, descendant of Wytchwood. Goodbye, Ryan Schilling.*"

With that, the voice of the ancient mathemagician faded away for the last time.

Ryan had reached the end of the corridor, and he

pressed the square stone in the wall. The door swung open and Ryan stepped outside. He found himself standing on the parapet once more, with his back to the marble wall. The door slammed shut behind him.

Ryan glanced at his watch. The policeman was staring down at him, red-faced and angry. "And look at me and not your watch when I'm talking to you," he was saying.

Ryan smiled. Not only was he outside the clock tower, but he was back at the exact moment before he'd pressed the stone.

"Get back down those stairs," said the policeman, gruffly. "And clear off."

Ryan turned and ran down the outer stairs. It was as though the wicked dance of chaos had never taken place – as though he had never been inside the Clock of Doom at all.

As he turned onto the final flight of steps, Ryan noticed the crowd of people grinning up at him.

"Hey, Ryan," came a voice from the back of the crowd. "Is that you? We've been so worried."

Ryan looked around. And there, waving his arms in the air, was Uncle Karl. He was standing between Aunt Ingrid and Marta Martine, with Max at his feet. Ryan bounded down the remaining steps and through the crowd to join them.

"Oh, Ryan," cried Aunt Ingrid, throwing her arms around him. "Thank heavens you're all right. Out all night in that terrible weather..."

"The forest can be a dangerous place at the best of times," said Uncle Karl. "But you look none the worse for wear." Max jumped up at Ryan and licked his hand. "We've been looking for you everywhere," his uncle added.

"When the Clock appeared I suggested that we might find you here," Marta Martine interrupted. "I explained to your aunt and uncle how good it was of you to bring me my *medication*."

"Well, yes," said Uncle Karl. "It was a kind thought, Ryan – but you really shouldn't have left the house." He slapped Ryan on the back. "The main thing is that you're in one piece. What a time to come to stay in Oberdorf. First the incredible snowstorm, now this strange clock tower and the sudden thaw. I've never known anything like it."

If you only knew, thought Ryan. If you only knew.

He glanced up at Marta Martine. A faint smile was playing on her bright red lips.

Ryan frowned, thoughtfully. There was something he still had to do.

The next morning, having asked his uncle whether he

could go for a little walk, Ryan set off once again in search of the site of the ancient hunting lodge.

He eventually found the concealed stairway, and followed it back down to the underground wine cellar. He found the right barrel and, with bated breath, he lifted the latch and pushed the door open.

The secret chamber was just as it had been the previous day. The flaming torches on the walls were still bright, the rows of apparatus were still in place and the cauldron was still bubbling. But the occupant of the chamber, Magoria himself, was nowhere to be seen.

Ryan called his name. There was no reply.

Gone, he thought. Had the ancient mathemagician somehow managed to leave his underground prison? Or had he finally died?

Ryan saw the book and the chart of *The Ripples of Time* lying on the table where he had left them. Beside them was something else – a letter, the words a spidery scrawl. It was addressed to him.

Thank you, Ryan Schilling,

Like Wytchwood before you, you were a true friend. With the crystal gone, thankfully, no man can live for ever.

Magoria.

Ryan looked up and found himself staring into the alcove. Of course, he thought. Something *is* different. The flame. The mysterious emerald green flame. It had gone – and with it, the ancient sorcerer.

Turning away, Ryan noticed a threadbare gown lying on the floor by his feet. He crouched down and touched it. As he did so, it – like the bones beneath it – crumbled to dust.

MORE CHILLING STORIES TO KEEP YOU AWAKE AT NIGHT

TERRY DEARY

The Boy Who Haunted Himself

There's no escape from the ghost in his mind.

ISBN: 9780746060360

MALCOLM ROSE

The Tortured Wood

Who will be the next victim?

ISBN: 9780746077436

ANN EVANS

The Beast

How can you kill something that's already dead?

ISBN: 9780746084595

SANDRA GLOVER

Demon's Rock

There's something evil out there...

ISBN: 9780746060377